stolen
wishes

a Wish I May
novella

stolen
wishes

a Wish I May
novella

by LEXI RYAN

Cover © 2013 Sarah Hansen, Okay Creations

Interior Design by E.M. Tippetts Book Designs

Editing by Rhonda Helms and Editing 720

dedication

For all my readers who loved Will and Cally and wanted to read more. This is their beginning and it's for you.

chapter one

Cally

"Come on, sweetheart." Kenny Riles edges forward, his snickering minions close behind. "I'll give you fifty dollars for a hand job. That's twice what I paid your mom."

I wrap my arms around myself, blaming the chill in the early spring night for the shivers running through me. I came to the dark stadium to be alone. Now, I'm wishing I had a friend with me. Hanna to wrap her arm around my shoulders, or Lizzy to crack a joke about the size of Kenny's dick before telling him to fuck off. The guys smell like beer, cigarettes, and a dangerous lack of inhibition.

Kenny's eyes sweep over me greedily. "You ain't out here for nothing. You're looking to suck a little dick, ain't you? Let's see if you're as good as your mom."

The sound of footsteps—a fast and noisy hustle up the bleachers—has me pulling my gaze away from Kenny's hazy eyes.

I can make him out in the moonlight—a figure in a hooded sweatshirt and athletic shorts running up the bleachers and down the steps, up the bleachers, down the steps, zigzagging his way closer and closer to us.

I've never been so grateful to see a jock in my life.

"I'll pass." I try not to let him hear how his words affect me. But fear lodges in my throat, making the words smaller than I intended.

Kenny grabs my hand.

"Back off!"

The clanking of feet on bleachers stops, and silence seems to echo through the stadium. "Get your fucking hands off the girl, Riles," the jock calls, coming toward us.

"What? She your girlfriend?" Kenny asks. "When did you start slummin' it, Bailey?"

Bailey? William Bailey. *Shit.*

Rich kid, golden boy, quarterback. And so very much the object of my fantasies. Really, universe? You couldn't have put *anyone* else here to witness my embarrassment?

"Does she have to be my girlfriend for you to understand what *back off* means?" William asks. He's closer now, his face dark and glowering.

"I'm just giving the girl some business, but I guess if you're her customer tonight, we'll get out of your way."

Hate boils up in my stomach, and I have to close my eyes. I can't look at William when this guy is implying such horrible things about me. I'm too scared to see his face, too afraid he might believe them.

"Come on, guys. Let's get out of here." Kenny and his guys exchange a few grunts and stomp away down the bleachers.

I inhale deeply for the first time in several long minutes and force myself to look at William.

"Are you okay?" He comes closer and pulls the hood from his head. His smile is cautious, worried. I can almost make out the warm blue of his eyes in the moonlight.

My stomach flips. Everyone in this town knows who William Bailey is. He's smart and popular and beautiful. Everything I'm not. "I was just leaving," I lie.

"You're Cally Fisher, right?"

That surprises me. We have one class together—third hour French—but he's always busy chatting with his friends. I never thought he noticed me. "Yeah…"

"I've watched you."

I raise a brow. "You've *watched* me?"

"Wow. Not like that." He chuckles and runs a hand through his hair.

He has these unruly blond curls girls go mad over, present company included. "Now I sound like a bigger creep than Kenny, don't I? I've *seen* you. You walk by the river a lot. I worry about you. You're always alone and it's always after dark."

"I like the stars," I answer, then immediately wish I'd kept the childish words to myself.

He shoves the sleeves of his hoodie up to his elbows as he scans the empty stadium. "Me too, but you shouldn't be out here alone."

"And where's *your* babysitter?"

That grin is back, and I feel like the luckiest girl in the world to have it aimed at me. Stupid but true. "Touché."

"Well, thanks for your help with the asshole squad. I appreciate it." I make myself head down the steps. After the day I've had, another ounce of kindness from him and I'm bound to make a fool of myself.

As soon as my feet hit the pavement at the foot of the bleachers, he's beside me.

I shift awkwardly. "You can get back to your workout or whatever."

"I could. Or I could use my chauvinistic concern for your welfare as an excuse to walk a pretty girl back to her house."

My cheeks burn. We walk in silence for a while, cutting across the dewy grass to get to Main Street, where the street lamps illuminate his face and make me feel self-conscious in my ratty old long-sleeve tee.

"So, do you want to talk about it, or would you prefer we continue with the romantic silence?"

I think he might be flirting with me. Which is just… No. There's no way. This is William Bailey we're talking about. He can have any girl at our high school, and probably a healthy handful of the girls at the university down the street.

"Talk about what, exactly?" I ask stupidly.

"About Kenny? Or the reason you spend more time after dark wandering around New Hope than at your house?"

"Kenny's just a jerk."

"Agreed. And the other?"

How do I explain my nighttime walks to a guy who has everything? The stars winking at me from the sea of black sky, the sound of the river, the whisper of the wind in the trees. In the crisp air, when everything is cloaked in darkness, I feel closer to the stars. No one needs me. No one sees me. No one taunts me. Looking at the stars and wishing for something better isn't just something I enjoy. It's necessary for my survival.

I wouldn't expect him to understand that.

"I like wandering at night." I shrug. I don't want to tell him about what drives me to seek haven in the darkness. Mom, lost in her pills. Dad, nearly as oblivious, lost in his books.

"You don't have to wander alone, you know. I mean, you shouldn't. Guys like Kenny look for any excuse."

My steps slow as we near the turn to my house. "Thanks for your concern. I'll see you around." I turn the corner, and he stays by my side as if I hadn't just dismissed him.

I stop and prop my hands on my hips. I don't want him coming any farther. He lives in one of the restored brick mansions near the center of town, and I'm too embarrassed for him to see the ramshackle doublewide trailer that's barely big enough for my family. "Goodnight, William."

"Oh, so you already know my name? I thought you just didn't care."

"*Everyone* knows your name. And *everyone* cares."

His eyes drop to my mouth. "*Everyone?*"

My heart slams against my chest and I think for one stupid minute that maybe he's going to kiss me, but then he takes my hand and tugs me toward my house. "Let me walk you home, Cally."

We amble slowly, as if neither of us really wants to reach our destination, my body romanticizing every second of this and buzzing with anticipation, while my pragmatic brain frantically denies any possibility that this guy—this *way freaking out of my league* guy—could possibly be attracted to me. He takes me all the way to my front stoop, and I when I turn to tell him goodbye, his gaze is on my mouth again.

William

My heart pounds in my chest. I'm nervous. Like a kid on his first date.

Cally has the biggest eyes and the softest lips. This isn't the first time

I've noticed. She's in my French class. She's quiet and always looks a little alarmed when Madame Layton expects her to speak.

"Thanks for humoring me," I whisper.

"What?"

"For letting me walk you home. I enjoyed it." I smile and squeeze her hand. Am I the only one who feels this electric pulse of energy when our hands touch?

I wasn't lying when I said I didn't think she cared who I was. She keeps to herself in class, her nose in a book unless she's whispering to the Thompson twins, who sit next to her at the front of the room. I've spent weeks watching the way she bites her lip as she takes notes. I know she lets that curtain of thick, dark hair fall in her eyes when she's trying to hide and which friends make her face light up when she smiles.

And I know the rumors about her mom, which were no doubt the reason Kenny and his crew were harassing her tonight.

My hackles are rising from me just thinking about the asshole leaning toward her on the bleachers, grabbing her hand. "Listen, about Kenny—"

"Don't worry about him. It's fine."

"It's not fine, and I won't let him say those things about you."

She frowns. "Why do you care?"

Because I have a wicked crush on you. Because I've seen you staring up at the night sky like you're looking for something you've lost, and I understand that more than you know. "Because Kenny's an asshole."

She laughs and her whole face lights up. "You can say that again."

I want to make her smile like that all the time. "My friend Max is having a party tomorrow night. His parents are out of town. Any chance I'll see you there?" I hold my breath while I wait for her answer. I shouldn't have asked, but I can't help wanting to see her outside of school. I can't help wanting a chance to make her smile again.

"Cally? Who are you talking to out there?"

I didn't even hear the front door open, but Cally's mom is standing on the porch in a thin white nightgown that's damn near transparent in the porch light.

Cally tenses and pulls her hand from mine. "Mom, go inside. You're not decent."

Her mom looks down as if she needs the reminder of what she's wearing. "He's cute. Is he your boyfriend?" Her words are just slurred enough that I'm not sure if she's drunk or half asleep.

"No, he's not." Cally's so emphatic I wince. She turns to me. "I have to go." Then she hustles to the porch, wraps her arm around her mom and ushers her into the house.

Standing in the quiet night, I can hear their muffled voices inside the house, but I can't make out what they're saying. I'm starting toward home when I hear the porch screen squeak open. I turn back, thinking Cally is trying to catch me, that maybe she wants to say more, but then she sinks to the stoop and looks up at the stars.

She's not out here for me. She's out here to escape whatever is inside that house.

She has no idea how alike we are.

chapter two

Cally

KENNY'S WORDS have clung to me like tree sap since he cornered me at the stadium. Thick and sticky and impossible to ever completely remove. No matter how much I try to scrub them away, their residue remains.

"That's twice what I paid your mom."

That's just something mean boys say. I know that. But I also know the looks Mom gets when she goes into town. Women who used to be kind to her now duck their heads and hurry in the other direction when they see her coming.

I told myself Kenny was just an asshole trying to show off for his friends. I told myself he was just trying to get a rise out of me, to see what I would do. But even if that's true, it doesn't mean he's lying about Mom. And even if I want to tell myself he's a liar, part of me already knew the truth about the state of her "massage" business.

And last night when she came onto the porch, barely decent in front of William Bailey, disgust roiled in my stomach. Now every time I look at her, all I can think is, *Did you take money to give Kenny Riles a hand job?*

"And Frankie said he would do it if she gave him her lunch," my little sister Drew is saying.

I blink at her, realizing I've missed half her story. I try to be a good listener for Drew. Someone needs to be.

"And so she did," she continues, "and on recess, *he did!*"

I fill her bowl with cereal and milk as she settles into her seat at the kitchen table. "Did what?" I ask.

"Ate a *worm*," she squeals.

"That's disgusting!" I wrinkle my nose, and she giggles. She's in first grade and generally a happy kid, despite everything. "Gabby," I call. "Want some cereal?"

Gabby hops up from where she was playing in front of Saturday morning cartoons. She toddles toward me. "With milk," she instructs in her little voice.

I settle her into the chair across from Drew and pour her cereal.

In the living room, Mom is sleeping on the couch, oblivious to our daily early-morning ritual.

"Cally eat?" Gabby asks, her mouth half full of cereal.

I shake my head. I can't handle the idea of food when Mom's purse is staring at me from the kitchen counter, her datebook inside.

My stomach flips when I think about what I might find there, but I have to know.

I leave the girls at the table, giggling about something they saw on a cartoon. The zipper seems to screech as I pull it open. I peek around the corner into the living room, but Mom is still sleeping. With a deep breath, I pull the black appointment book from her purse and leaf through it. Last month, last week. I scan over the scribbled names and I'm almost relieved.

Then I see it. Thursday afternoon. *Kenny.*

I snap the book shut quickly, as if staring at his name next to 4:00 might show me more than I want to know about their appointment.

"Can I have a Pop-Tart?" Drew asks.

I shove the book back into Mom's purse and zip it up, pushing it to the back of the counter where I found it. "No Pop-Tarts. There's enough sugar in that cereal."

"My have Pop-Tart?" Gabby asks. She's talking a lot for her age, but she always substitutes "my" for "I." It's ridiculously cute.

"How about an apple?"

The girls groan, but I grab a knife from the drawer and an apple off the counter.

So what? Kenny got a massage from Mom. That doesn't mean he got anything *more* than that. Does it?

I slice the apple into two bowls, removing the peel from Gabby's half. I'm handing the bowls to my sisters when my father emerges from the bedroom.

"You ladies are up early." He pushes his glasses up his nose and attempts to smooth his bedhead. He probably fell asleep reading in his recliner again.

"This is pretty much the normal time," I mutter.

He rubs his hands together. "I think it's a good day to go book shopping in Indianapolis. What do my girls say?"

"Yay!" the girls chorus.

"I think I'll pass," I say. I'm too preoccupied with the whole Mom and Kenny thing to enjoy a rare day with my dad. The girls will have a good time. Dad goes to these big used bookstores where the girls can get half a dozen new books for under five dollars. Of course, Dad will likely spend too much, buying more books about Taoism and Buddhism and any other -ism that promises to make sense of the universe. But the time with Dad is good for the girls, and the time alone will be good for me.

Mom shifts on the couch. "Cally? Are the girls up? Do they need anything?"

I close my eyes and bite back my frustrations. She wants to be a good mom, just not more than she wants her next fix. "It's okay. Go back to sleep."

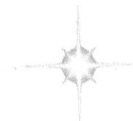

"I HAVE a problem."

Lizzy Thompson crosses her arms and looks me over disapprovingly. "That you do. I can't believe you kept this from me."

I shift awkwardly on the steps of her front porch. I don't even know what she's talking about, but I'm freezing out here. "Are you going to invite me in or leave me out here?"

She pulls the door open wider, and I step into the warmth of her foyer. Blood finds its way back to my frozen fingers, making them burn.

I pull off my coat, and Lizzy takes it and throws it on the banister before grabbing my hand and dragging me upstairs to her room.

Hanna is lying on her stomach on the floor, leafing through a magazine. When she sees me, her eyes go big. "Is it true?"

"Is what true?" I look back and forth between my two best friends, waiting for them to explain.

"She would have told us," Hanna says to Lizzy.

"Not necessarily," Lizzy replies. "Maybe it was an impulse thing and this is the first chance she's had."

"*She* is standing right here," I mutter. "Tell me what you're talking about."

"We heard you and William Bailey were together at the football field last night," Hanna says, pushing herself off the floor.

"That's true, I guess." I shake my head at the worry on my friends' faces. "I don't understand. What's the big deal?"

The girls exchange another one of those knowing looks. They may not look like it—Hanna with her long, dark hair and Lizzy with her blond curls—but they're twins, and it can be a little creepy how much they can communicate with each other without speaking.

"People are saying you were *together*. In the bleachers," Hanna says.

Lizzy rolls her eyes. "No, they're saying you were *fucking* in the bleachers."

My jaw goes slack, and I stumble back and lower myself to sit on the edge of the bed. I should have seen this coming. William was just trying to protect me, and what does he get in return? A bunch of rumors that he's nailing the poor chick with the slutty mom. God, he must hate me.

"Do you look so horrified because your secret's out or because it's a lie?"

"Lizzy!" Hanna screeches.

"What? Tell me you haven't thought about it. How many times have we placed him in the top five hottest guys in New Hope?"

Hanna's cheeks flare red, and she sinks next to me on the bed. "Ignore her. You don't have to tell us anything, but we thought you should know what people are saying."

I shake my head again. It hasn't even been twenty-four hours, and rumors are already making their way back to my friends. "Who told you that?"

"Krissy told Meagan who told us," Lizzy answers. "But Krissy won't say where she heard it."

"Kenny Riles, no doubt," I mutter.

"Why do you say that?" Hanna asks.

"Kenny's gotta be mad. Will put him in his place last night."

Lizzy narrows her eyes. "Put him in his place before, during, or after he made hot monkey love to you?"

"He didn't—"

"Don't!" She puts her finger to my lips. "Please don't tell me it didn't happen. Not yet. Not while I'm still looking forward to living vicariously through you."

"You're ridiculous." Hanna giggles. "But not wrong. I'll admit to having a stray fantasy or two about William Bailey myself."

"Just *one or two*?" Lizzy says. "He pushed up his sleeves in French the other day, and just looking at his forearms inspired at least seventeen different fantasies that day alone."

"He's taken!" I hear their older sister Krystal holler through the wall.

Lizzy shakes her head. "Don't mind her. She's had a crush on William since they were in eighth grade and thinks he's hers, but he's not into her."

The girls make me chuckle, despite myself. "I'm sorry to say you won't be living vicariously through me today. Nothing happened between me and William on the bleachers."

With a sigh, Lizzy sinks to the bed on the opposite side of Hanna. They lean their heads on my shoulders, squishing me into a twin sandwich.

"Kenny was out with his friends," I explain. "They were drunk, and he was trying to...proposition me, I guess? He said he'd bought a hand job from my mom and wanted to know what *my* going rate was."

The girls gasp in unison.

"He didn't!" Hanna whispers.

Lizzy growls, "What a fucker."

"It was actually kind of scary," I admit. "But then William was there, and he told them to leave me alone. They left, and Will walked me home. End of story."

"Kenny is such a creep," Hanna mutters. "But you need to tell Will so the rumor doesn't take him by surprise."

I nod. Talk about an awkward conversation. *"Hey, when you go back to school on Monday, everyone's going to think you shagged me on the bleachers. Sorry 'bout that."*

"It won't change anything," Lizzy warns. "But I agree it's better if he knows."

"I'm sorry he said that about your mom," Hanna whispers. "He's such a nasty liar."

I swallow hard and nod, remembering Mom's appointment book. *Had* Kenny been lying?

Time to change the subject. "I guess I need to talk to William," I say. "You know, he mentioned a party at Max Hallowell's tonight. Would you two be up for that?"

Hanna claps gleefully. "We'd love to come with you!"

"Han!" her sister says. "We can't be there when the *obvious* solution is for Cally and Will to do the nasty so the rumor is the truth."

chapter three

Cally

"THANKS FOR coming with me tonight," I say to the girls as we walk up the steps to Max's house.

Hanna smoothes her hair. "Yeah, going to a party at Max Hallowell's house is such a hardship."

"We aren't staying long," I promise, more to give myself courage than because it's what they want to hear. "I want to give William a heads-up, and then we can get out of here."

"Oh, let's not rush away," Hanna says. "We don't want to insult the host."

"Do I sense a crush?" Lizzy asks.

Hanna's cheeks pinken as she knocks on the door. "No crush. He's a nice guy, end of story."

"A nice guy who just broke up with his girlfriend," Lizzy singsongs.

The door flies open, and a sleek-haired blonde stares at us skeptically. "Can I help you?" No, she's staring at *me* skeptically. I think her name is Kristen if I remember correctly. We had gym class together last semester, and she made a few cracks about my cheap wardrobe in the locker room. I might have *thought* a few cracks about her slutty wardrobe.

"This was a bad idea." I turn to leave. This isn't the place for me.

"Cally."

The sound of William's voice calling my name has my feet stalling on the steps. Lizzy squeaks beside me as I turn around. No one ever made jeans and a T-shirt look as good as William does. The dark denim hugs his hips, and the white T-shirt shows off his sculpted chest and shoulders.

"You came." He steps outside and grabs my arm, ushering me into the house.

"Um, yeah. These are my best friends, Lizzy and Hanna," I say awkwardly.

"Yeah, I grew up with all the Thompson girls. They lived next door to my grandma until their mom built that house on the river." He gives them a polite smile before turning back to me. "I'm glad you decided to come. You can throw your coats on that couch over there."

The girls and I peel off our jackets and toss them on the couch, and when I turn around, William is running his gaze over me. I'm wearing jeans and one of Lizzy's sweaters. It's black and fitted and shows more cleavage than I'm normally comfortable with, but Lizzy talked me into it. She also did my makeup, defining my eyes with dark liner and mascara and topping the look off with a swipe of lip gloss. Now I'm glad I let her fuss over me. I like the way his eyes linger on my curves and lips before returning to meet mine.

"You look gorgeous."

"You—you too." Damn. He's so sweet, and I'm just so…awkward. "Hey, can we talk?" Better to rip off the Band-Aid.

He smiles. I'm dazzled by that smile. It shoots something electric through my veins and back to my heart.

I look to my friends, not wanting to leave them before they find their place here. New Hope parties can be cliquey, and not in a good way.

"Go!" Lizzy urges. "We're fine."

I sink my teeth into my lip and nod.

William takes my hand and leads me to the stairs. A few catcalls go up as everyone watches us climb them together. Great. This is the exact opposite of what I came here to accomplish.

"You do fast work, man," someone calls, and someone else says, "Protection is in the bathroom."

By the time we're on the second floor, my cheeks are burning with embarrassment and shame. Embarrassment over the things those guys probably think we're doing up here. Shame for bringing that down on Will.

William leads me into a bedroom just off the stairs and shuts the door behind us. "I'm sorry about Sam and Max," he says softly. "They don't mean any harm. They're just jealous because they couldn't get a girl alone upstairs if they tried."

I shake my head. "I'm the one who's sorry. They're all going to think we're having sex up here."

He chuckles and brushes my hair from my face. His callused fingers set my skin to life, and I want to feel more of them. I imagine them tangled in my hair as he lowers his mouth to mine. I imagine the way they'd feel skimming over my neck. Lower.

"I don't think any of my friends really believe I'm that lucky," he says with a wink.

"You haven't heard yet, have you?"

His face turns serious. "Heard what?"

"Kenny Riles is telling everyone that we—" I swallow hard, my cheeks blazing with a new wave of embarrassment. "He's saying he saw us having sex on the bleachers." Then I add the new detail the girls learned before we left their house tonight: "He's saying you paid me."

Will steps back, his hands balling into fists, his jaw going tight.

"I wanted you to hear it from me first. I'm so sorry."

"Why do you keep apologizing? It's not your fault Kenny's a piece of scum who has to make shit up to feel like he serves a purpose in this world."

"I don't want to hurt your reputation."

He narrows his eyes, then his whole face softens and he steps close again. "You're serious, aren't you? You're worried about *my* reputation? What about yours?"

I lift a shoulder in a half-shrug. "My mom pretty much screwed up any chance I had of having a pristine rep."

He draws in a breath, like he's shocked I said it out loud. I guess I'm a little surprised too.

"I'll do whatever you need to fix this," I promise. "But we should probably start by getting back downstairs so we're not fueling the gossip mill."

"Maybe we should start by getting down there and dancing."

"Dancing?" I can't think straight when he's this close to me. The only thing dancing with William is going to accomplish is making me crush on him that much harder. "How is that going to help?"

He takes my hand and squeezes my fingers. He draws me toward him until my mouth is just a breath from his. Then, his lips curving into that charming, knee-melting smile, he reaches around me and opens the door. "Follow me."

Almost everyone is too preoccupied with their own conversations to notice our return, but Will's buddy Max spots us and shakes his head. "Stamina, man. You gotta work on the stamina if you want the beautiful ones to stick around."

"Cut it out, Max. Cally, this is my idiot best friend, Max. Max, this is Cally, my *guest*." He says the word like it has some sort of secret meaning then slides his hand around my waist and tugs me close.

Max's brows shoot up and he gives a knowing nod. "Say no more." He has a nice grin and he shows it off as he offers me his hand. "Nice to meet you, Cally."

"You too," I say, but the words come out as a whisper. I'm still tangled up in the sensation of Will's arm around my waist.

"I saw you brought your friends." Max nods to Lizzy and Hanna. They're at the island in the kitchen, laughing about something.

"I hope that's okay."

He lifts a brow. "Are you kidding? Beautiful girls are always welcome in my house."

"Max has a thing for Lizzy," Will whispers in my ear.

Max punches him lightly in the stomach. "Hush it, man." Then he turns to me, serious. "But do you happen to know if she's…available?"

Crap. Hanna's the one who likes Max. "Um. I don't think so. I mean, she doesn't seem really interested in more than just, you know, friends and stuff."

"Figures," Max says with a heavy sigh.

William takes me to the makeshift dance floor at the back of the living room and pulls my body next to his. I recognize the song as Nine Inch Nails' "The Fragile." I love this album. Hanna and Lizzy tease me for listening to it, but something about it has always spoken to my heart.

"You don't mind, do you?" His words are lazy puffs of air at my ear.

"Don't mind?" Wow. His presence seems to take away my ability to construct complete sentences. *Real attractive, Cally.*

He pulls me closer and settles a hand at my hip. "Dancing with me," he whispers. "Pretending to be my girl?"

I pull back so I can see his eyes, but they're all serious and expectant as he waits for my reply. God, he's gorgeous.

I don't know what to say, so I don't answer at all, just move with him to the music. His hand slides from my hip to under my shirt, his thumb against the sensitive skin above the waistband of my jeans.

"Hey, William," a girl calls from the kitchen. "Why don't you come in here and take a shot?"

I hardly have a chance to tense before Will pulls me closer. "Can't do that, Meredith. My date's here."

Lizzy and Hanna both turn to us at his words, and I feel my own eyes go wide.

"I'd consider it a personal favor if you could roll with this," he whispers into my ear. "Meredith has been trying to get me to do body shots since she got here two hours ago."

"You don't drink?" I ask, not that it's my business. I've just never been to a party with alcohol before, and I'm not sure what to expect. From the stories I've heard, I half expected everyone to be wasted by the time we got here.

"It's not the drinking that I mind. She's just not my type." When I frown at him, confused, his lips quirk in a half-smile. "You do know what a body shot is, don't you?"

I shake my head.

"Want to find out?" His fingers trail over the sensitive dip in my spine as he asks, and I nod. I would probably agree to anything he asked me right now.

He takes me to the kitchen, his hot hand never leaving the small of my back.

Lizzy and Hanna step back and study us as he leads me to the island. I'd feel guilty about abandoning them tonight, but they seem to be having a great time.

"Where's the tequila, Max?" Will calls.

Max hoists a bottle of amber liquid in the air and snags a shot glass off the counter.

"Do you know what a snakebite is?" Will asks me quietly. He's standing close so only I can hear him when he talks.

I bite my lip. "I don't really go to many parties."

Next to us, Max fills the shot glass with tequila.

"A snakebite is a shot of tequila that you take with salt and lime," Will explains to me.

"What makes it a body shot?" I ask.

His throat moves as he swallows, and his blue eyes go darker somehow, his pupils getting bigger. His lips part as he studies mine. "It's a body shot if you take all the parts of the snakebite off someone else's body."

That makes my pulse kick up a notch. I'm still trying to puzzle out the logistics when Max calls, "No hands, Bailey."

Will winks at me. "And I can't use my hands for anything but putting the salt on you. Are you still game?"

I nod wordlessly, and I'm rewarded with one of Will's full-out grins. I don't need to know details to understand his mouth is going to be on me, and I like the idea of that. A lot.

Will's hands slide to my waist and tighten, and before I realize what he's doing, he's hoisting me up on the counter. I squeak, and the girls cheer. All of them except Kristen and Meredith, that is. They're leaning against the fridge, scowling at me like I killed their puppy.

Max hands me the shot glass and looks at me expectantly.

"Do I hold it?" I whisper.

"If you want," Max says. "But I think you shouldn't make it so easy on my boy here."

Will shakes his head. "Whatever you're comfortable with."

Lizzy rushes over and cups her hand around my ear. "Slide it between your breasts. Trust me."

I gape at her, and she shrugs innocently before joining Hanna at the edge of the kitchen.

I may be inexperienced, but I'm not naïve and I get what this game is about. My cheeks heat as I slide the glass into my cleavage. It's cool against my hot skin, and Will's eyes burn into me as he watches me position it.

Max offers me a lime wedge.

"Do you need your friend to tell you what to do with that too?" Kristen calls.

"Shut up, Kristen," Will says. "You didn't know what you were doing your first time either."

But she's right. Lizzy shouldn't have to tell me what to do. I take the lime and put it between my teeth, facing out. The citrusy pulp presses against my lips, making them tingle. Or maybe the tingle is from the idea of William's lips close to mine.

Will grins and brushes my hair off my neck. "Ready or not."

When his hot tongue hits my neck, I'm assaulted by shivers of pleasure so potent I'm embarrassed to have all these people watching me. Instinctively, I tilt my head to the side to give him better access to my neck.

He nips the skin before lifting his mouth to my ear. "Still good?"

I can only nod.

"Good." He sprinkles salt onto the spot he just wet with his tongue, then licks it off and brings his mouth to the tequila. Since I'm on the counter, he doesn't have to lean down far, but he takes his time wrapping his lips around the glass. His face is practically buried in my cleavage, his breath hot against my breasts, and my cheeks burn with embarrassment and arousal.

When he comes up with the shot and tosses it back, I offer my open palm to take the glass. His mouth closes around the lime, and he holds there for two heartbeats, his eyes closed.

When he pulls away, he takes the lime out of his mouth and licks his lips. "Thanks for that." He brushes my cheek with his thumb, eyes locked with mine.

We hang there for a moment, not moving or breathing, time suspended as our eyes lock. It doesn't matter that there are at least a dozen other people in the room. For that moment, with his gaze equal parts hot and tender, I don't even care what they must think of me or what rumors might or might not be circulating when I return to school on Monday.

"Shit!" someone says. "Did you hear that thunder? It's going to rain!"

"Bailey," Max murmurs by Will's side, "can we get a little help moving the couch back into the house before it's destroyed?"

"I'll be right back. Don't go anywhere." He winks at me, then disappears out the back door.

"Well, *that* was hot," Lizzy says, offering her hand to help me off the counter.

"So hot," Hanna agrees as I hop down. "I'd be jealous if I weren't so happy for you."

"Same here. Crap." Lizzy winces. "I shouldn't have broken the seal earlier. I need to pee again."

"I'll go with you," Hanna says before turning to me. "You okay?"

"I think so." I put my hands to my blazing cheeks. "I just need a cold drink."

Lizzy snorts. "I'll bet you do. We'll be right back." Then the girls are gone.

For the first time, I look around the kitchen and living room to survey the other party guests. Several of the guys rushed outside at the threat of rain, but the house is still pretty crowded, more so than when we arrived. There's a couple not two feet to my left who may need protection if they dance any closer, and another in the corner practically dry humping.

I look around the kitchen and find a cooler with bottles of water. I really just want to stick my face in the ice for about ten minutes, but this will have to do.

"Look who decided to close her legs for a few minutes," someone snipes as I come up with a bottle. It's Kristen, and she's scowling at me.

"Excuse me?"

"Listen. I know you're just trying to climb on up the social ladder. Heck, if I were a social pariah, I'd do the same. I'm just gonna do you a favor and spell this out for you before you have to learn the hard way. William Bailey can have any girl he wants. Money, good looks, status, Will's got it all. There's only one reason he'd go out with a girl like you. And I'm pretty sure he just showed you what that was."

Anger surges inside me. "You don't know anything." When are Lizzy and Hanna going to be back from the bathroom? I could use some reinforcements about now.

Kristen shrugs and pours herself a shot of tequila. "I'm not judging you for doing it. Hell, I'd fuck him until he couldn't see straight if I had the chance. But I can work in his world, whereas you'll just get hurt if you try. But maybe I'm giving too much credit to a girl who gives it up on the bleachers."

"Who told you that?"

She smirks. "Will was bragging about it to his boys right before you got here."

chapter four

William

"So, Cally Fisher, huh?" Max says for my ears only as we push the couch back into position in the living room.

I shrug. I like Cally. A lot. But I'm not about to say anything definite to Max until I know the feeling is mutual. It's gotta be, though. The connection between us it too intense to be one-sided. Damn, my blood still runs hot in my veins when I think about the smell of her skin and the little shiver that ran through her when I pressed my tongue to her neck. I want to think she enjoyed that as much as I did. "I don't know yet," I say, scanning the crowd for her face.

Meredith sidles up to me and rubs against me like a cat. "You can do better than her," she purrs in my ear. "Come upstairs with me and Kristen and we'll show you just how much better."

"Give it up, Mer," I say, nudging her away. The last thing I need is for Cally to see one of these drunk girls throwing themselves at me like they give a shit. All they care about is what I can do for their reputation. Or worse, what my money can buy them. I'm so over that kind of girl.

I go to the kitchen, but Cally isn't waiting for me there. She's not in the living room, and she's not dancing.

I glance down the hall and see a long line of girls waiting for their turn in the restroom. Maybe that's where she went. I wonder if I can get her back upstairs. I want to talk to her without all these people watching us. I want to put my lips on her neck again without the excuse of alcohol.

I hated leaving her, but Max's parents would shit if they found out about this party, and how else would he explain a couch left out in the rain?

The feel of a small, cold hand under my shirt has me spinning around. *Cally.*

But it's not her. It's Kristen, and she's grinning up at me like the cat that ate the canary. "Guess your little date couldn't handle partying with the cool kids?"

"What?" I push her hands out from under my shirt. "What are you talking about?"

Kristen rolls her eyes. "Cally and her friends left while you were out back with the guys."

Left? *Shit.* "Where'd she go?"

"Maybe her mom needed help jacking off a client."

"Grow up," I growl. I rush out the front door and down the steps before Kristen has a chance to say more. Cally is walking down the sidewalk with the Thompson twins.

For a split second, I'm torn between following and letting her go. If she doesn't want to be here, I'm not going to make her. But the look in her eyes after I licked her neck has me jogging down the steps after them.

"What's going on?" I ask when I reach them.

The twins exchange a look, then turn to Cally. "Do you want to talk to him?"

She bristles, but nods slowly. "I'll catch up."

The girls nod and cross to the other side of the street, tossing worried glances over their shoulders as they walk away.

What the hell did I miss?

Cally

"WERE YOU just going to leave without saying goodbye?" William tucks his hands in his pockets, and there's something more reserved about his body language. As *he's* the one who's been hurt here.

I thought William was better, different than other guys. But what do I know? Just because I'm attracted to him and he has a sexy smile doesn't mean I should assume he's better than the average horn dog. Heck, maybe that's why he isn't worried about the rumor. How do I know he didn't start it?

Even as I think the question, I know the answer. I know he didn't start the rumor because there's a goodness in his eyes that can't be faked. But is that enough of a reason to trust him?

I want to erase the last twenty minutes, to go back to the dance floor when I believed he might actually want me for me. But I'm not that stupid, and I can't let myself be.

Suddenly, in the war between my body and brain, my brain wins. And my brain is furious.

"I'm not a slut." The words drop like mini-grenades from my lips, detonating the minute they register with him and obliterating that invisible pull between us.

"Excuse me?"

I shrug. "I'm not stupid. I know there's only one reason a guy like you wants to spend time with a girl like me, but you have the wrong idea. I'm not like that."

"A guy…" He draws in a long breath, his jaw ticking. "A guy like me?"

"Money, good looks, status?" I say, using Kristen's words. "But I'm not going to be your easy lay. If that's what you're after, you should go talk to the girls inside. I'm sure you'll find some takers."

He steps back, pain flashing in his eyes. "I would think that someone who struggles with people's assumptions about her would be more careful about making them about others."

"What am I supposed to think?"

He looks up at the dark sky and laughs, a hollow, disappointed sound. The clouds obscure the moonlight and only the distant streetlight reveals his face.

I feel the icy rain hit my cheeks before I see it. Then it's coming down faster, stinging my face as we stare at each other.

His jaw is hard and he shrugs. "Forget it."

My stomach tightens in disappointment. What did I expect him to do?

"Catch up with your friends before they get too far," he mutters. "I don't like you walking alone in the dark." Then he turns and jogs back to the house, and I'm left feeling like a world-class bitch.

William

"YOU READY to talk about it yet?" Max asks me as we head to the cafeteria for lunch on Monday.

"Talk about what?" I've been in a shit mood since Saturday night, so I can probably guess.

"Who pissed you off, for starters? Or maybe why you skipped out on my party so early?"

I feel my jaw go hard at the mention of the party.

"Ah, so it *is* girl trouble," he says.

"You're worse than a woman. Mind your own business."

"Didn't work out with Cally?"

I scan the notifications on my phone, buying time while I think of how to reply, how much to share. Cally and I are from different worlds. There's a division between the Haves and Have Nots. Even in a place as small as New Hope—*especially* in a place as small as New Hope. And especially in this school. But maybe that's part of the appeal. Maybe I like Cally so much because she's outside my typical circle.

"It wasn't because of what Kristen said to her, was it?" Max asks. We stop at his locker, and he turns the dial and yanks it open before shoving some books inside.

I scan the lunchtime crowd gathering in the space between the cafeteria and the glass enclosure around the pool. Cally has the same lunch period as me, but she doesn't always come down. "What did Kristen say?"

Max shrugs. "You should probably ask Cally. I wasn't there so I didn't hear it, but Ally said Kristen was feeding Cally shit about you only wanting her for one thing."

I wince. "And she didn't say anything?"

He shifted uncomfortably. "She didn't know what was up with you and the Fisher girl, so what could she have said?"

"Nothing is *up* with her. We're friends."

Max grunted. "You looked like a lot more than friends when your face was buried in her tits."

"Fuck off." The suggestion doesn't carry much weight when my heart isn't in it.

"So, you didn't leave with Cally, I'm gathering?" He slams his locker shut and we start toward the cafeteria again.

I sigh. "She took off. Told me there was only one reason a guy like me would be interested in a girl like her." The words have an entirely different meaning now that I know Kristen was talking shit.

"And you let her go?"

I take a deep breath and stop, leaning against the wall. I'm not up to eating today, though my football coach would be on my ass if he knew I was skipping meals. "It was a bitchy thing to say."

Max nods. "Can't argue with you there. But given her mom's reputation and what Kristen said to her, you can't blame her for being cautious."

"I guess."

"Goddamn Kristen," I grumble, my eyes still scanning the crowd for Cally. "What was she thinking?"

"Probably that if you were going to be using someone for sex, she wanted it to be her."

"Well, she's already given me that opportunity. I passed."

Max shoves his sleeves up his arms. "Damn. Must be tough to be you."

I shrug, not about to explain the truth—that I don't want to be the guy girls like Kristen pursue so viciously.

"There are rumors," Max says, averting his eyes. "I don't know if you've heard them. Rumors that you paid Cally to have sex with you."

I drag my hand over my face. "Yeah. I know."

"And if she's not even talking to you anymore, it's only going to fuel the gossip."

"Do I look like I care about rumors?"

"That's why you're better than the rest of us." He slaps me on the back and pauses a beat. "You're not going to tell me if they're true, are you?"

My head snaps up. "Cally is not a fucking prostitute. Jesus."

"Easy, killer!" He holds up both hands and shakes his head. "I know you didn't *pay* her. I'm just wondering about the other part. But you're too classy to tell me. Never mind."

"We didn't have sex. She's not like that." I spot that long, dark hair at the entrance to the auditorium. And Kenny. "Damn it."

"Good luck with the girl," Max calls as I rush away.

"He's done with you," Kenny's saying when I get close. "I'm just waiting my turn."

Cally's arms are wrapped around her middle and her face has gone pale. "I don't have sex for money."

"So you're trying to say there's something between you and the rich boy? Because it's pretty clear to the rest of us what you are to him. And when he—"

Kenny doesn't get to finish, because I'm spinning him around and slamming him against the wall, my forearm pressed into his neck. "What's that you're saying, Riles?"

Kenny scowls at me. "Thought you were done with her, man."

Fuck. No wonder Cally thinks the worst of me. That's what everyone is telling her to think.

"You're lucky I don't beat the shit out of you," I say in his ear.

"Bailey!" I hear the teacher's voice and back off Kenny, dropping my arm and releasing him. "What's going on?"

"Nothing." I force a smile. "Just having a little chat."

"Let's keep it that way," she says, but she walks away, too sure of my reputation to stop her patrol.

Kenny shakes his head. "She's not worth it." Then he walks away.

When I turn back to Cally, she's staring at me. "Thank you," she whispers. "I guess you're kind of my knight in shining armor lately."

I nod. "No problem." I start to walk away.

"William."

The sound of my name off her lips stops me in my tracks, and I turn back.

"I'm sorry," she says softly. "I should never have believed what that girl told me. You're a nice guy, and it didn't add up. I should've known better than to think the worst."

She looks so sweet standing there, guilt all over her features, and my heart is still slamming in my chest from seeing Kenny bearing down on her like that.

"Let's put a stop to these rumors," I say without thinking. "Go on a date with me this weekend. I won't let everyone think I just used you for sex." Or *worse,* paid her for it.

"Oh. Um…" She sinks her teeth into her bottom lip, then nods as her cheeks flame red. "Right. Sure."

"I'll pick you up on Friday at six."

Cally

I DON'T feel sorry for myself very often. Maybe I should. My family doesn't have money, and I've never been able to dress like the kids at school. When I was ten, I had to quit dance lessons because we couldn't afford them anymore. I loved dance more than anything, but I understood quitting was a necessity so I never cried about it. Never complained.

My dad taught me to be grateful for the things we do have. A roof over our heads—better than some can say—a family to come home to, and the free will to dream up and go after whatever life we want.

But tonight, I'm thinking of William Bailey and having quite the pity party. I'm thinking about Kenny and his snickering friends and wondering if a pity date with William is really going to solve anything. But mostly, I'm just wishing my mom were different.

She's at the computer when I head out into the living room to confront her. Dad bought a bunch of used components at a sale at the college and pieced together a computer that's supposed to be for my school papers, but Mom uses it more than I do. I don't know what she does on there. I once told myself it was work for her business, but I don't believe that anymore.

"What are you doing?" I step up behind her. She's got some sort of realty site pulled up and is looking at pictures of houses.

"Ever wonder what it would be like to start over?" Her voice is slurred and I spot the glass next to her. Looks like orange juice, but Mom doesn't do OJ without vodka. And she's probably taken her pills since she got home. In other words, it's four p.m.

"Not really," I lie. Because I have thought of it. How could I not? But I don't want to have some fanciful conversation with her while she's like this. I frown at the photos on the screen. She must be drunk. We could never afford a place like that.

"I'm going to make it happen," she says, as if reading my thoughts. "I'm going to find a way for us to start over. To live large for once." She takes in a deep breath, a woozy smile half curling her lips as she lifts her glass for a drink.

I don't normally feel sorry for myself and I don't normally hate my mother, but right now I'm disgusted with her. *Just say it.* "Did you give Kenny Riles a hand job?"

Her glass clatters down on the old desk, and she spins to look at me, blinking. "Who's Kenny?"

I wither right there. Like a flower shoved into a dehydrator. Like a star blotted out by the clouds. Not "What are you talking about?" but "Who?"

"I go to school with Kenny. He said he paid you twenty bucks for a hand job."

She draws her bottom lip between her teeth and chews on it. Her eyes are glassy and she tilts her head to the side. "The name doesn't ring a bell. Is he one of my clients?"

I try to laugh but it sounds wild and crazy, and then suddenly my stomach is crawling into my throat and I can't stand it anymore. I rush to the bathroom and throw up.

I squat hunched over the toilet, listening to the once-comforting sounds of Mom running cold water. My stomach is empty by the time she places the cool cloth on my neck.

"I have an appointment Friday," she says. She hands me a plastic My Little Pony cup filled to the brim with water. "Can you watch the girls? I think your dad has a meeting."

An appointment. She just all but admitted that she does sexual favors for her clients—though I think she's oblivious to what I gleaned from the conversation—and now she wants me to watch the girls so she can meet with one of them? *Fuck no.* "I have a date," I say. "I guess you'll have to cancel your appointment."

She frowns. "A date? Who's the boy?"

"William Bailey." I lift my chin. I know she'll recognize the name, and I want her to understand that not everyone who lives in this house has sold out. I want her to know that nice boys still want to be with me.

Even if it's not exactly true.

"Oh, sweet Cally. What do you think a Bailey wants with you? Don't give it up to him. Your dad was so sweet to me when I was your age and I got pregnant. Look what became of my life. Don't let him steal your chances for a good future."

I clench my fist because I want to slap her. The only one who's stolen my chances is standing right in front of me.

chapter five

William

"MAKE SURE you save room for dessert," the waiter says.

The little restaurant is in a restored brick mansion on the New Hope square. Candlelight illuminates our white-clothed table and reflects in Cally's deep brown eyes.

She's nervous, and it's the most adorable thing I've ever seen. She pushes her food around on her plate and studies me through those thick lashes when she thinks I'm not looking. I noticed her the first day she walked into French class this semester, all that dark hair hanging past her shoulder blades, her eyes guarded when someone talked to her.

Does it make sense to say that I felt instantly connected to her, long before we ever had a conversation? She was a girl who understood loneliness the way I did, who didn't want anything from me.

I picked her up at six, just like I promised, and she was waiting outside for me, no doubt to make sure I didn't go into her house.

I wish she weren't so self-conscious about her home and her family. I don't care that she doesn't have money. I have more than I'll ever need, and I hate it. I'd trade every penny to have my parents back for a single day.

"Did you want dessert?" I ask.

"No thanks."

I want to reassure her that I'm paying for this and she can order whatever she likes, but the words would only make her more self-conscious. Instead I order the chocolate lava cake, and when it comes, I pull my chair around the table so it's next to hers.

The dark chocolate cake steams, the ice cream on top already melting. I cut into the center with my spoon. Gooey, melted chocolate rushes out.

Her tongue darts out to wet her lips. "That looks amazing."

I scoop a bite—making sure to get cake, melted chocolate, and a bit of ice cream all onto the spoon—then I offer it to her. "Try it."

I slide the bite past her parted lips, and pleasure lights up her face. My breath catches at the sight, and I immediately prepare another spoonful, then another.

When I offer the fourth bite, she puts her hand to her mouth and shakes her head. "It's your turn," she insists.

"I'm good."

She licks her bottom lip but misses the smudge of chocolate just beneath. "Then why did you order it?"

Cupping her chin in my hand, I wipe the chocolate off with my thumb. Her lips part and she's so close I can feel her breath as it rushes past her lips. I want to kiss her. Damn. I can't believe how badly I want to kiss her. Instead, I say, "Go for a walk with me?"

She nods, and after I pay the bill, I lead her out of the restaurant and toward the path along the river, linking my fingers through hers as we walk. The night is clear and the stars shine bright, their pinpoints of light reflecting off the water. Cally looks up at the stars and her whole body seems to soften. I feel the tension rush out of her with her sigh.

"Thank you for tonight," she says. "Most guys wouldn't have gone to such lengths because of a stupid rumor."

"You think I wanted to date you to satisfy the rumor mill?"

She focuses on the pavement in front of us, avoiding my gaze. "Didn't you?"

"You're not that naïve, are you?" That gets her to look at me. Her eyes are narrow and frustrated. "Cally, I took you to dinner tonight because I wanted to. I don't like what they're saying about you, but my reasons for asking you out were more selfish than they were noble."

She stops and leans one shoulder against the trunk of a thick maple as she studies me. "How were they selfish?"

"I wanted a chance to have some time alone with a pretty girl."

She stares at me for two heartbeats. "I really like you, William Bailey."

I tuck a lock of hair behind her ear then shove my hands in my pockets to keep myself from touching her more. "I like you too, Cally Fisher."

Her teeth sink down into her bottom lip and her eyes drop to my mouth.

I fist my hands in my pockets and exhale slowly. "I really want to kiss you right now."

"I really want you to," she whispers, flicking her eyes to mine.

I take a cautious step forward and press my hands against the tree trunk on either side of her head, then slowly lower my mouth until it's a breath above hers. "Has anyone ever kissed you before?"

"Yes."

Jealousy burns in my gut. It's silly, but it's there at the thought of another guy touching his lips to hers. "Who?"

"Davey Mills kissed me on the lips behind the school in second grade." Her eyes flash with mischief and she bites back her smile.

"Lucky Davey," I grumble. "Must have been memorable."

"Yes. He kissed me during a game of truth or dare. I remember he had peanut butter breath."

I chuckle, and her face breaks into a full-out grin. I close the breath between us and brush my lips over hers. Unlike Cally, I have some experience with this, so I'm surprised how much it affects me. Just a kiss. An innocent connection of lips. But the contact is electric and it sends a shockwave of pleasure through me.

I slide my hand into her hair, and she opens under me, meeting the sweep of my tongue with the hesitant touch of hers. She tastes like sweet tea and makes this soft little sound at the back of her throat. I break the kiss before I'm ready because my hands itch to touch her, to slip under her shirt and cup her breasts, to slide around her hips and squeeze her ass. She's not ready for that, and I won't rush her.

Her tongue darts out and skims over her lips. "Come with me."

She takes my hand, and I follow her farther down the path and along the river until there's a break in the trees. She leads me onto the grass and sits on the ground.

I sink to my haunches and settle beside her, the dew seeping into my jeans.

"Lie back." She leans on her elbows and points to the sky. "This is my favorite spot."

We settle onto our backs, bodies aligned, fingers entwined, and look up at the stars. From this spot, the sky is all I can see, and it feels like I'm being swallowed up in it.

"Tell me something no one knows about you," I ask into the silence. It's probably a stupid request, but I don't care. I like her and I want to know more about her.

"Like what?"

"Tell me what you wish for when you look up at those stars."

She's quiet for a long beat, then another. When I hear the whoosh of her exhale, I think she's not going to share anything, but then she says, "Lately, I've been wishing that my parents would get a divorce."

That surprises me, and I roll to my side to look at her as she speaks.

She winces but continues. "They make each other miserable, but instead of facing it or doing anything about it, they both hide. It's the worst possible thing for my parents." She faces me and forces a smile. "Pretty boring stuff, isn't it?"

I trace the worry lines around her eyes until they relax. "It's not boring at all. It's real." The girls I know are so proficient at being fake, they could give lessons. Cally is the opposite of fake. She's authentic.

"I just think they could be happier, you know? And maybe coming out here and making wishes is juvenile, but I like to think of it as throwing positive energy into the universe and hoping it comes back something better."

"You're not like other girls, Cally."

She rolls her eyes. "You say that like it's a good thing."

"It's so refreshing. You have no idea." I slide a hand into her hair and kiss her again. This time, I linger. Our lips brush, our tongues rub, and before I know it, she's on her back and I'm on my side, pulling her body close to mine and resisting the instinct to slide my thigh between her legs.

She keeps her eyes closed for a long time after I draw back, and I'm struck for the thousandth time by how beautiful she is. Dark hair. Pale skin. Rosy lips. "I should get home," she whispers.

I nod, but I stay there looking at her for a few more beats. She doesn't rush me, doesn't seem uncomfortable sitting in the silence.

When walk back to her house, I take her the long way, through town, knowing everyone will see us and talk. Wanting them to.

Cally

THREE WEEKS and six amazing dates, and William Bailey doesn't seem bored with me yet.

The gossip mill isn't giving up on us entirely. There's all sorts of speculation as to why a guy like William would spend so much time with a girl like me. But the worst of it has died down. Apparently, the possibility of us having sex in the bleachers isn't nearly as juicy if we're actually dating.

He showed up to my house tonight and asked my dad if he could take me on a walk. It was the sweetest thing, though my dad looked a little puzzled by it. We find ourselves down by the river again, the early spring breeze ruffling our hair, the sun loosing its grip on the edge of the horizon.

"This is my favorite time of day," Will whispers.

I lean against him and sigh. "Sunset?"

"No." He reaches over and slides a hand into my hair. "The part where I'm next to you." Then he brings his mouth down to mine and kisses me softly.

I live for these kisses. These happy moments between the craziness at home, the demands of the girls, and the stress of school.

"You are beautiful. You know that?"

"Hmm," I say. "I'm not sure. Tell me again?"

"You." He presses a kiss to the corner of my mouth. "Are." Another kiss right under my earlobe. "Gorgeous." His hand slides up my side until his thumb is brushing the underside of my breast.

That light touch feels so good, and I arch into it, even as my brain screams it's time to pull away. He lowers his mouth to mine and kisses me until I'm breathless. My body wants more, but I'm terrified of what it will mean if we go further. I need to know I'm enough. To know I'm not my mother.

"I'm sorry," I whisper, pulling back. "I can't."

He leans his forehead against mine and closes his eyes. He's breathing heavily, and I like that I can do that to him. I like it too much.

When he pulls back and looks at me, he says, "I didn't mean for that to happen. I'm sorry."

"I'm not ready."

"You don't need to be ready for anything. I just got a little carried away."

"It's not that I didn't like it. It's just…" I draw in a shaky breath and force a smile. "I liked it a lot. I like kissing you, but that's all we can do, and I'd understand if that meant you didn't want to date me."

He stiffens and turns toward the river, resting his forearms on his knees. "Not all guys are shallow jerks who only care about the physical stuff."

"I don't think that of you at all," I protest. "But I want to be fair to you."

"Then give me a chance," he says, turning to me. "Be my girl, Cally. I don't want there to be any confusion about what we are to each other."

My stomach flips at the idea, and I can't figure out what I could have done to deserve someone like him. "Did you miss the memo?"

The breeze floats by, and I can smell him. Boy soap and aftershave. It's a scent I could snuggle into and drift away on.

"What memo?" he asks.

"The one that says the quarterback is supposed to date the head cheerleader?"

"Hmm. I've dated a cheerleader before. It's pretty much overrated. Though"—he drops his gaze to my legs—"I wouldn't complain if you wanted to wear the uniform."

I swat him, and my hand stings when it connects with his solid chest. "Ouch."

"That'll teach you to hit me."

I giggle, then admit, "I like that idea."

"Oh, the uniform."

"No," I squeak. "Of…being your girl. But I need to tell you something first."

He brushes my hair from my face and traces the line of my jaw, his eyes following his finger. "What's that?"

"That night Kenny was harassing me at the stadium?"

His body tenses. "I remember."

I swallow. I need him to know more than the rumors. I need him to know the truth. "He said he'd gotten a hand job from my mom."

"Jesus," he hisses. "He's such an ass."

I pull my lip between my teeth and chew on the corner before confessing, "I don't think he was lying."

"Why would you say that?"

"We don't have much money. My parents are terrible with it, and then there's not much coming in and…" I take a breath, wondering if I dare say the rest out loud when I've never even told Hanna and Lizzy. "My mom's been taking Vicodin since Gabby was born."

"Did she have some sort of complication?"

I shake my head. "No, she just…likes it. She hides in her pills. I don't know where she gets them, but I have no doubt in my mind that her addiction is to blame for at least part of our money trouble."

"I'm sorry."

"She's always had this little massage business, but it's changed in the last couple of years. The ladies don't come to her anymore, and people whisper about her. About what she does. The worst part is that I think the rumors are true. I think she got desperate and…" The truth is too sickening to put into words. "Are you sure you want to get involved with me?"

"I don't care what your mom's done. I only care about you."

"When I say I'm not ready, I don't just mean tonight. I don't know if I'll be ready next month or next year. It's not that I don't want to, but I'm scared I'll become her."

His breath leaves him in a rush. "Never. You'll never be her." He pulls me close, and I move to straddle his lap.

"You seem so perfect. I don't know what being with me is going to do to your life."

"My life is hardly perfect," he scoffs. He holds me close while he lowers himself back into the grass. He's silent for a bit, my head on his chest, his hands toying with my hair. "I was young when my parents died. I have memories of them, but nothing big, you know? My memories are more like snapshots. My dad handing me a big present in Garfield birthday wrap. Mom sweeping me off the ground and kissing my bloody knee. Sitting in the back of the car and watching the two of them hold hands. I wish I had more but it's just not there."

I wrap my arms around him and squeeze because that's all I can do. There's nothing to say to salve the hurt in his voice. Nothing to do but listen.

"I was in kindergarten when they died in the accident, and I don't remember much about that time. I was staying over at Grandma's that night, and Mom and Dad were having 'couple time.' Grandma said it with disapproval in her eyes, so I thought 'couple time' meant something bad until I was older and heard other people use it." He pulls in a breath not much different than the kind I take when I wake up from a nightmare. "They never came home."

"I'm sorry," I whisper. It physically hurts me to imagine little-boy Will waiting for his parents to get home, wishing he'd see them again and learning he wouldn't.

"Grandma didn't like to talk about it. She took me to the funeral, dressed me in a suit and tie, and told me, 'We get one day to cry. After today, we move on. You become the best man you can and you do it for them.'"

"That's terrible. Grief shouldn't have a timeline. And you were just a kid."

"She loves me. I don't want you to think any differently. But her loving me meant that she didn't want me hurting, and if she didn't have to see me hurting, she could tell herself I wasn't."

"What was it like? Growing up without your parents?"

His hands, already in my hair, tighten before he speaks. "I had everything I needed, so I don't want to make it out worse than it was."

"You can tell me."

"It sucked." He forces a laugh. "I love my grandmother, but she wasn't a mother to me. She didn't know how to be, not when she was so filled with grief over losing her own son. She wanted so much for the son she'd lost, and I was expected to fill that void. The grades, the sports, the perfect behavior. I need to get out of here for college. She wants me to go to Sinclair, but I know what that means. She'll want me to live at home. She'll want to control how I spend my days."

"You could go anywhere, do anything."

He hooks a leg behind mine and rolls us until he's on his elbows hovering over me and his lips are a breath from mine.

"What are you thinking?" I ask.

"That I can't wait to tell everyone you're my girl."

Then he kisses me for a long time, slow and sweet. We look at the stars after, side by side, his fingers tangled in my hair. Then we see it. A shooting star, skating across the sky as if it were put there for us.

I can't help but wonder if my time with William will be like that. A precious but temporary gift.

chapter six

William
Eleven Months Later

"Open it!" Cally says, her eyes bright. She's grinning at me, and we both know very well what a fat envelope from a college means.

"I don't want to." I chuck it to the floor and nudge her backward until the bed hits the back of her thighs. She's so damn beautiful when she smiles. Just the idea of not seeing that smile every day makes me want to scrap all my plans for college. Ten months ago, the idea of getting a fat envelope from Notre Dame would have sent me over the moon. When it came today, my first thought was of the long drive between here and there. "There's one more application I'm waiting on." I slide my hands into her hair.

She frowns. "From where? I thought you'd heard from everyone already."

"Sinclair."

She presses her hands against my chest and pushes me back. "No. William. No. Absolutely not."

I hang my head. This is why I hadn't told her. I knew how she'd feel about me sticking around for her. "I don't want to leave you."

"But you need to," she protests. "You need to get away from your grandmother and have a chance to live your life without her constant meddling. You told me that's what you wanted, and I think it's what you need."

I grab her hand and bring it to my lips. "That was before you."

Her eyes fill with tears. "I can't let you do this. I love you too much."

"I love you too," I whisper, then I dip my head to kiss her.

"Don't change the subject," she whispers against my lips.

"I wouldn't dare." Our mouths meet again, and I sweep my tongue across her lips until she opens for me and makes that little kitten mewl at the back of her throat. I nudge her again, and she lowers to the bed, her dark hair fanned against my blue sheets. "You're so beautiful."

She's wearing cut-off jean shorts that show her long legs, and one of my old practice jerseys. Her back arches as she reaches for me, and the jersey slides higher, revealing a narrow strip of creamy skin right above the waistband of her jeans. The part of me that loves her and understands her hang-ups resists, but there's a part of me that's ready to push, a part that wants her too much not to ask for more.

I know my friends think we have sex. Hell, other than Cally and me, I don't know any couples who aren't sexually active. But we have more than they do. We have a connection that I've craved since my parents died.

When Cally's around, I never feel alone.

Cally

OVER THE clothes and above the waist. That was my line in the sand at the beginning of our relationship. Lately, it's a line I want to kick myself for drawing.

When we first started dating, I kept waiting for the other shoe to drop. It's not that I'm a pessimist or something. It's just that William is so much more than I ever would have imagined for myself. He's not just the sexy football player everyone loves. He's smart and kind and thoughtful. And when I told him I wouldn't have sex with him, he took me at my word and has never pushed the physical side of our relationship. We make out, and when things start to get too heated, when I'm ready for him to ask for more, he slows us down and pulls me back.

Over the clothes and above the waist. My rules, followed to a T.

Stupid rules.

I complained to Lizzy and Hanna about my predicament, and Lizzy laughed at me. "So, strip. You show him some bare skin, and I'm sure he'll get the idea."

I was going to wait for our one-year dating anniversary. But lying here in his bed, no one else in the house, my body has other ideas. The way he's looking at me right now gives me the courage I need. I sit up, and before I can talk myself out of it, I pull my shirt off over my head.

His breath draws in with a hiss and his gaze sweeps across bare stomach, my breasts swelling above the cups of my bra. "You don't have to do this if you're not ready," he says, but his eyes give him away. He needs this as much as I do. "Cally, I—"

I unclasp my bra, and he stops talking, his chest rising and falling as his eyes rake over me again and again.

"Jesus. You're beautiful." He wraps his hand around my side and pulls me close, lowering his mouth to mine.

His fingers are gentle. He sweeps them over my bare skin, cups a breast in his palm. I gasp at the brush of his callused hand. He's touched me here before, and I always liked it, but this is different. There's no comparison, and this simple contact makes me want more. Skin to skin, everywhere.

"So damn beautiful." He drops his mouth to my neck. Pleasure jack-knifes through me when he rolls my nipple between his fingers and scrapes his teeth over my collarbone. "Let me kiss these. Let me make you feel good."

I'm almost tense, coiled tight and needy, waiting for his mouth on my breasts. I want to feel his tongue against the sensitive flesh of my nipple. He kisses the sensitive crook of my neck and teases me with his thumbs. What will it feel like to have his mouth there? What if I don't like it?

"Relax, baby." He lowers me to the bed and runs his hand across my abdomen. His fingers dip into the hollow of my navel then up between my breasts. He follows with his mouth, hot and wet against my stomach,

43

his tongue skimming under the band of my jeans and sending wild flutters through my belly before he kisses his way back up.

By the time he brings his mouth to my breast, pleasure twists inside me, greedy and impatient and more intense than anything I've ever felt before.

His tongue circles my nipples, one then the other. He closes his mouth over the taut peak and sucks, his other hand pinching the opposite breast.

The spiral of desire pulses harder, more insistent, and I squeeze my thighs together tight as he teases and sucks. I cling to that sensation—the tight, twisting ache. I tug at his hair because I need more, and I'm so close to something but I'm not sure what it is. Suddenly, he sucks again, and that aches twists impossibly tight before shattering and rocking through me in a violent spasm of pleasure.

I cry out, and he sucks harder until the spasm recoils and releases again, and I'm arching into his touch, holding on to his hair and the back of his neck.

Finally, my body lightens and releases, and I drop my hands to my sides. When I open my eyes, William is looking down at me, his blue eyes hot, his face searching mine.

When the realization of what I just did clicks into place in my sluggish brain, my cheeks burn with embarrassment. I held his mouth to me like I was afraid he was going to stop. I—*Oh my God*. Who has an orgasm from a guy touching her above the waist? "I don't know why that happened. I'm sorry."

He smiles but it looks a little pained. "Are you seriously apologizing for the sexiest thing I've ever experienced in my life?"

"I… You thought that was sexy?"

His lips quirk. "Baby, I made you come just by kissing your breasts. Not only was it sexy, I feel like Superman right now."

"Superman?"

"Maybe Houdini is a more appropriate comparison, but yeah." There's so much intensity in his eyes that I can practically feel the weight of his gaze as he runs it over me again. "You've pretty much made my life."

I bite my lip. "It's a little embarrassing from where I'm sitting."

He draws me up against him and nuzzles against my neck. "God, there's absolutely nothing for you to be embarrassed about. The only thing embarrassing here is the way I'm about to come in my jeans without you even laying a finger on me."

"Really?"

He groans. "You have no idea how much I want you. It hurts like hell."

That sobers me, and I pull away. "William, I'm sorry I—"

"Please don't apologize. It's a good kind of hurt."

I guess I know what he means. I've been feeling the good kind of hurt for months. I'm just not sure how much longer I want to feel it. My gaze drops to his jeans before I realize what I'm doing and tear my eyes away. I looked long enough to see some very impressive tightness at his fly that wasn't there earlier.

He pulls off his shirt and snuggles next to me, wrapping his arms under my breasts and pulling me close. "Let me hold you like this," he whispers in my ear.

I breathe in his scent and my eyes slowly drift closed. The sun slants in through the window and warms my skin, relaxes my muscles.

I'm nearly asleep when he says, "I love you, Cally."

I'm getting used to hearing those words. He told me for the first time months ago, and I was in awe that someone as amazing as William could love me. I never doubted his words. They are like him—honest, pure, and easy. But when he first said them, I was struck by the vulnerability in his eyes. I used to think William had everything, but I was wrong. He didn't have love. Not as much as he deserves. And maybe his grandmother's love for him is unconditional, but he can't see it when she puts so many conditions on her approval. My parents might suck at being parents, but I've never doubted their love. I would never have guessed that William needed my love more desperately than I needed his.

"I love you too," I reply softly now.

"If I leave for school, will visit me? Will you wait for me?"

I twist, turning in his arms so I can see him. "Notre Dame isn't that far. A few hours on the bus, and I'll be there."

Relief washes over his face and he slides his hands into my hair and pulls me close for a kiss. When he releases me, I settle into his chest again. "Thank you," I say—to him, to the universe or whatever desperate stargazing wish brought us together.

chapter seven

Cally

He forgot.

I wrap my arms around myself and pace my bedroom. I can't believe he forgot.

My phone rings, and I practically jump across my bed as I scramble to grab it.

I don't bother to read the display. "Hello."

"Hey, chica!" Lizzy says from the other end.

My shoulders sag in disappointment, and I look at the clock. It's after eight p.m. "Hey, Liz," I mutter.

"Any word from lover boy?"

"He texted me to let me know his grandma had roped him into a card game and he'd try to stop by later."

"He's with his grandma!" she howls, outraged.

"No way!" I hear in the background. Hanna, no doubt.

Normally, I wouldn't be bothered by Will playing cards with his grandma instead of spending the evening with me. Because William is just that kind of guy. He plays poker with his grandmother and her friends every week or so. I've never gone (though he's tried to convince me on several occasions), but from what I gather, the women get rowdy drunk and play a cutthroat game.

But it's our one-year anniversary, and I had hoped for more. I'd planned for more. I guess this is what I get for not reminding him of the date. Honestly, I didn't think I needed to, and it hurts, realizing how wrong I'd been.

"You need to call him and let him know how disappointed you are," Lizzy says. "If you don't, I will."

"Please don't." I walk over to the window and look outside, half expecting to see him waiting with roses and a smile. "It's not that big of a deal."

"Liar," she says.

"You know how his grandmother can be. I'm sure she laid on quite the guilt trip, and he didn't feel like he could leave her."

"But it's your *anniversary*," Lizzy whines.

The sound of dishes crashing echoes down the hallway from the kitchen. Shit. Mom must be cooking drunk again. "I have to go," I say quickly. "I'll call you later."

"You better," she says.

I hang up and slide the phone into my pocket before heading to the sound. I'm met in the kitchen with the sight of my mother putting dishes into boxes. My heart skitters to a stop. "What are you doing?"

"I'm packing." She looks up at me and smiles. It's a real smile. Not one of those Vicodin-laced plastic ones. Her eyes are clear, like maybe she's sober for the first time in months. "You girls and I are about to begin an adventure. A new life in Las Vegas."

"What are you talking about?" Maybe she is high. She's not even making sense.

"In a few weeks, we're moving to Las Vegas. Aren't you the luckiest teen in the world?" She grins at me like she really believes what she's saying.

"I'm not moving anywhere. My life is *here*. You can't seriously expect me to just throw away everything because you want to follow some whim."

Glass clatters as she slams the platter she's holding onto the counter. "This isn't a whim. This is me taking control of my life, making something of it. That's what you told me you wanted, right?"

"I didn't mean—"

"You know, your sisters are excited. Don't ruin this for them."

My sisters are too young to understand what moving away means. "What about Dad?" I manage.

She winces then hides her face behind tissue paper as she resumes packing. "He's the reason this is happening. He wanted to quit his job and go on some spiritual quest in Bali. I decided it was as good a time as any for us to divorce. We haven't been happy together in a long time. This divorce is giving us what we both want."

"Well, I'm staying here." My voice sounds pathetic, desperate.

"You'll love it in Vegas. The lights, the excitement. It will be a fresh start for all of us. Everybody wins." Her smile doesn't look so sure anymore, though.

"Except me," I whisper. "I don't win. I don't *want* a fresh start."

"Well, it's time you grow up enough to understand things aren't always going to go your way."

Fear sits like a stone in the bottom of my stomach. It leaks its toxins into my limbs, making my arms and legs heavy. I can't move. I'm frozen in this spot until she fixes what she's broken. Until she unsays what she just told me.

"Don't look at me like that. I deserve happiness too."

"You're hijacking my life. You get that, right? You're taking something good and destroying it for your own purposes. That's the opposite of what a mother is supposed to do."

Her eyes fill as she stares at me, and I feel like I've just slapped her. "I know I haven't been a good mother, but I've done what had to be done. The girls at the bowling alley told me what the boys at school said about you, the rumors they spread."

"One boy spread one rumor. It's over now."

"I know that's my fault. I'm doing something right for once. I'm cleaning up and fixing my life. I've met someone and I'm ready to move on. So either help me pack or go to your room."

"You're going to change your mind," I say, maybe more for myself than her. "Packing is a waste of time."

I wander back to my room in a daze and shut the door behind me. The soft knocking on my bedroom window pulls my attention from my thoughts. In the darkness, I can barely make out William's face on the other side of the glass.

My chest hurts at the thought of leaving him, but I push the ache aside—there's no way Mom's going through with that—and hurry to open the window. "You have something against the front door?" I ask.

He grins. "I didn't want to wake up your sisters."

Just the sight of him makes me feel better. His smile warms me all the ways down to my toes, and I return his grin as his fingers lace through mine.

"How was poker night?" I ask, determined not to let my disappointment from earlier ruin our time together tonight.

"They're still going, but I excused myself after a couple hands."

"By which you mean you'd already lost all your money to the sharks?"

He chuckles. "Maybe I lost on purpose so I could see my girlfriend."

Oh, God. It's silly and childish, but I don't think I'll ever get tired of him calling me that.

"Do you want to come in?" I ask. I want him to.

"Nope. I want you to come with me."

I squelch my disappointment and climb out the window to join him. I'd been thinking of locking the door and lying with him in my bed, touching, kissing, letting things go too far. I'm ready to go too far.

He helps me hop down from the window and onto the grass. Unlike when we started dating at this time last year, the weather has been warm. And tonight the sky is so clear, the thick crescent of moon is enough to light the night.

"I missed you." He steps closer and places his hands on my hips before lowering his mouth to mine. His kiss starts patient and slow. When I fist my hand in his hair and press my body against his, it changes, growing hungry and impatient. When we break the kiss, we're both breathing heavily.

"You sure you don't want to come into my room?" I say, grasping on to my courage before it fizzles away. "You could lie down with me." *On me.* The idea of the weight of his body on mine sends a shiver through me. The good kind that has my imagination on fire.

He groans, fingers curling hard into my hips. "You're killing me, Cally. If I didn't know better, I'd think you wanted me to break your rules."

"Rules were meant to be broken."

He blinks at me. "Are you sure?"

Am I? My heart slams in my chest. Nerves. Anticipation. Desire, low and heavy in my stomach and sinking to between my thighs. What if this is my last chance? What if Mom is serious about Vegas?

He kisses me hard, his hands tightening their hold. "I don't need everything. I just need you."

I turn to lead him back to my window, and he stops me.

"Not here." He pulls a silky black necktie from his pocket and offers it to me. "Put this on?"

Laughter slips so unexpectedly from my lips that I throw my hand over my mouth, afraid I might have woken the girls. "Aren't we missing some steps between kissing and bondage?"

He steps toward me and takes the tie from my hands, settling it around my eyes. "Trust me." He presses a kiss to my nose, and then he's taking my hand and leading me—somewhere.

"Okay, but I'm just going to tell you now that I don't think we're ready for handcuffs yet."

His soft laughter mingles on the night air with the song of the frogs. "Where are we going?"

"Patience, grasshopper. You'll see soon enough."

I'm quiet for what feels like forever as we walk. Nerves knot in my belly and every so often he squeezes my fingers. I try to guess where we are from the turns and the sounds of traffic, but New Hope after dark isn't exactly a hopping place.

Finally, we stop. "We're here," he says.

"Hmm. And where's here?"

He releases my hand, and I feel him press a kiss to the top of my head. "Stay right there."

I listen carefully as I wait. I can hear him rustling around with something. Maybe the tinkling of glass. Something clicking. And then, behind all that, I make out the water splashing softly against something. I grin. "We're at the river."

"Don't go ruining my surprise," he murmurs as he releases the tie on my blindfold. When he slides away the fabric, I open my eyes.

"Oh."

We're on an old boat dock behind one of the closed factories on Main Street, and he's laid out a picnic on the concrete. Atop a red-and-white checked blanket sit two fat pillar candles. Their flames wink against two empty wine glasses. A glass serving platter is piled with crackers, cheese, grapes. Next to it sits a bottle of light pink liquid. "Is that wine?"

He grins. "Don't tell Grandma, but I snagged one of her bottles from the basement. It's strawberry." He takes my hand. "Join me?"

We settle onto the blanket, and he takes a slice of pear and tops it with soft cheese. Bringing it to my mouth, he whispers, "Try it."

My lips close around his fingers as I take the bite into my mouth. His blue eyes grow darker, smoky, and he goes for more. I let him feed me. Grapes, olives, cheese, crackers so thin and buttery they melt on my tongue. Every bite is a decadent discovery, and somehow his feeding me seems more erotic than kissing.

When he stops to pour the wine, I look around. I can see why he brought me here. It's the perfect view of the river and, above it, the stars.

"What did I do to deserve this?" I ask.

He hands me a glass. I drink, smiling when the sweetness explodes on my tongue. I've never had wine before, and I like how it sends warmth sinking into my belly.

"This is your reward for putting up with me for twelve months."

He remembered.

My chest tightens, like there isn't enough room to contain this feeling growing there. I don't know what to say, so I kiss him. I press my mouth against his and slide my fingers into his hair. He tastes like fruit and strawberry wine, and I move closer as our tongues touch.

When he moans against my mouth, I break the kiss.

I wait until his eyes open and then lift the shirt from my head. I set it to the side and watch him in the light of the candles and the moon as he takes me in.

"I'm sorry it took me so long to get to you tonight," he says. "I wanted to get everything set up. I wanted it to be perfect."

"It is."

He pulls at my hips, and I lie back on the blanket, bare to the moon and stars and to William's hungry eyes. He sips his wine and gives me a mischievous grin before tipping his glass and spilling a little puddle of it on the flat of my stomach. The liquid runs in cool rivulets over my belly and down my sides, but he dips his head and opens his mouth to the puddle. His tongue is hot, and shivers race through me as he licks away the sticky liquid, leaving my skin damp and hot in the night air.

I need to tell him about mom, about her packing, but I don't want to believe what she told me, and telling him makes it too real. Tonight, being here with him is all I need. Giving voice to my mother's crazy ideas would ruin everything, so instead I say, "Touch me."

William

"Rules were meant to be broken."

I don't think I've recovered from her speaking those words. Because the only thing I've wanted more than to break her rules was for her to ask me to.

Sliding my hands slowly up her thighs, I part her legs and kneel between them on the blanket.

"Come here," she says, reaching for me.

"I'll get there. Be patient." I circle her navel with my thumb, watching her face as the sensation whips through her. Her eyes float closed and she arches toward my touch. Then I replace my thumb with my mouth and trace an invisible path across her belly. She gasps, lifts her hips, and draws up her knees. I love that I can do this to her, love how she responds so completely to every touch.

I slide my hands up her torso and cup her breasts. They're so beautiful and I want her out of that bra so I can suck her nipples into my mouth.

"Cute," I murmur, running my fingers over the soft cotton of her bra. Cally likes underwear, so the Thompson twins bought her a whole load of it for Christmas. Some cute, some silky, some lacy. Watching her pull each piece from the gift bag after Christmas had made me lose my mind as I imagined what it would look like on her. This bra is covered with little penguins wearing top hats. "I'm guessing the underwear matches?"

Her eyes flash as they connect with mine. "Hmm…maybe you should find out."

My heart trips in my chest. I want to take off those jeans and see what she looks like in her panties. I want to cup her between her legs. To feel her there. I want more. "Are you sure?"

She lifts her hips. A tease. An invitation. A request.

Leaning forward, I press my mouth against her collarbone and kiss my way down her body. Placing an open-mouthed kiss over each nipple, I suck at her through the cotton until she cries out. I kiss along her ribs and over her navel. And when I reach the button on her jeans, I watch her as my shaky hands unbutton. I keep my eyes on her deep brown ones and draw the snug denim off her hips and down her legs.

"They match," I whisper, taking in the little penguins decorating the thin strip of white cotton between her legs.

"William?"

I swallow. Hard. I just want to lean forward and kiss her there. Open my mouth against the cotton. I want to explore that sexy strip of skin where her inner thigh meets this private piece of her, and then I want to slide my tongue under her panties and taste her. "You're so beautiful."

I graze my fingers over her stomach and down to her panties, my touch whisper soft as it reaches the apex of her thighs. My patience is rewarded with her cry, so I keep my touch light. "I want to make you come like this." My voice is rough, threaded with need.

She lifts her hips again, pressing into my touch. Then she surprises me by sliding her hands to her hips and pushing down her panties. "Please."

"Oh, damn," I murmur, but I peel off her underwear.

She's bare and exposed to me, and I can hardly breathe. I want to spend hours looking at her, but I can tell by the way she's shifting under my gaze that she's uncomfortable with this. I draw my body up until I'm lying beside her. She kisses me, and I'm lost in it for a moment. The sweetness of her breath, the soft glide of her tongue.

My hand slides between her legs and I gasp, swallowing her breath. I would give anything to know what it's like to feel myself inside her.

She shudders under my touch, and I still.

"Are you scared?" I hate the thought.

"Yes." She smiles at me and tangles her fingers in my hair. "But not scared about this. I just… I think sometimes I'm still afraid I'm going to lose you."

"You have me. I'm not going anywhere."

She closes her eyes.

"Is this okay?" I ask, circling that sensitive spot between her legs.

"If you don't mind."

I press my face into her neck and groan. "Why would I mind touching a piece of heaven?"

chapter eight

Cally

I WANT to touch him, make him feel like he makes me feel, but I have no idea what I'm doing and—

"Let's get you home, beautiful," he says, cutting off my thoughts. He gathers the plates, empties the glasses, and wraps up the food, placing it all back into his backpack.

I swallow back my disappointment. His grandmother is hardcore about his curfew—unlike my parents, who act like they've never heard the word. I fasten my bra and slide into my shirt.

He walks me home, touching me the whole time, like he's afraid I might disappear. At the front door, he kisses me softly. "Goodnight, Cally."

"Goodnight. Thank you for tonight. It was amazing."

He looks down at me and grins. A blond curl falls into his face. "You can say that again."

As I watch him walk away, something nags at me. In my dark house, I make my way to the shower. The nagging remains as I undress and step under the hot spray of water.

I told him I was ready to move forward, to do more, but I wasn't. I mean, we physically did more together, but I haven't truly moved forward from my previous position, from my fear that my worth to him would be tied up in giving him pleasure. Until I touch him, the fear won't release me from its grasp.

I dry myself off and hurry to my room with my phone to send him a text.

I'm sorry I didn't return the favor tonight. I should have. I think I'm scared.

I send it before I can overthink it and change my mind. I didn't have to wait long for his reply.

I don't want you doing anything that scares you. Anyway, now I have something new to think about while I take care of myself.

For a second, I'm not sure what he means by that, but then I understand, and the realization of his meaning causes something to stir in me. My nipples tighten. I never would have imagined the idea of a guy doing *that* could turn me on, but when I imagine William…

I hesitate, then type, *You…do that?* It's not that I don't believe it. He's a guy with a girlfriend who doesn't put out. Of course he does *that*. But I don't want to change the subject. Not yet.

His reply comes fast. *Don't you?*

My stomach flips and my heart kicks up a notch. I don't know what to say. I've never talked about this with a guy before. The girls joke about it, but this is different. I'm careful with my reply. *I guess. When it's necessary.*

And when's that?

I shift uncomfortably in my bed. If we keep up this conversation, it's going to be necessary very soon. *After a heavy makeout session sometimes. When I'm lying here wishing I were brave enough to do more with you.*

My heart pounds in my ears as I wait for his reply.

Damn. I didn't expect you'd actually tell me.

My cheeks burn, but even embarrassed, I'm not sorry I told him. I want more of this conversation. More of him. So maybe next time he's close to me, I'll find the courage to touch him in return. *Does it make you uncomfortable?* I type. I like that idea—him shifting in his bed thinking about me like I do him.

I grab my phone greedily when it buzzes with a reply. *I want you twenty-four seven. I'm uncomfortable as hell, and it's worth every second.*

Are you sure you're okay with waiting? I type quickly. *Just until prom. Then I'll be ready.* As I hit send, I realize I want him to say no. I want him to tell me he needs me now and doesn't want to wait anymore. I want him to show up at my window again, but this time I want him to come inside.

But his reply is even better than that fantasy. Because I know he means it.

I'd wait forever for you, Cally.

"WHAT ARE you doing?"

Dad is packing books into a small suitcase when I walk in the door after school. There are two more suitcases at his feet.

"Cally." He looks at me for a long time before saying more. His face is sad, those dark eyes, so much like mine, a little desperate. "One day, you'll be older and you'll understand that sometimes we just have to do things, even if not everyone in our life will understand or approve."

"It's true? You're really going overseas? You're leaving us?" In the weeks since I've caught Mom packing, she's mentioned Vegas a few times, but never with any definitive plans. I've let myself believe that and the half-packed house meant the move wasn't going to happen.

He doesn't answer but drops his gaze to his hands.

"You can't do this." My words sound panicky. Wild. "She's going to make us move, and that's not fair. My life is here. I don't want to leave."

"I'm sorry," he says to the floor.

"Cally!" Drew's voice comes from her bedroom and she shuffles out and wraps her arms around my leg. "Come play Barbies with me?"

"Daddy has to go now, Drew," my father says, nearly choking on the words. He squats to his haunches and opens his arms for her.

Tears burn the back of my eyes.

Drew runs into his arms and wraps her arms around his neck. "Bring me back something cool," she demands. "And maybe next time I can go with you."

"Maybe," he manages, but Drew seems oblivious to his emotion.

Gabby toddles out from the bedroom next, and Dad scoops her off the ground and nuzzles the side of her neck. She squeals with delight.

"I'll call," he says. "And if you want to move back here with me when I get home, let me know."

Drew frowns. "Cally's going to Las Vegas with us. She can't live here with you."

"We're not going to Las Vegas, Drew," I scold, as if it's her fault my parents have lost their minds.

"Yes we are. We're leaving at the end of the month."

My heart plummets, falling far past my stomach, past the floor-boards, and deep into the dark and fiery part of the earth. "No."

Mom wasn't failing to say anything about the move because she'd changed her mind. She wasn't talking to me about it because she didn't want to argue. And waiting until the last minute to pack the house? That's just her M.O.

Drew's eyes light up. "But you should come to Las Vegas, Daddy! Mom says it's a super fun place."

She can't comprehend the permanence of my parents' separation. Maybe it's for the best.

"I need to get to the airport," he says quietly, settling Gabby to the floor and picking up his suitcases. "You girls be good."

He heads to his beat-up old hatchback, and the girls rush to the window to wave at him as he goes. They don't understand. Or maybe he's been absent enough in their lives that they truly don't care. I don't know.

I watch his car back out of the driveway, and I feel like he's taking part of me with him. Not because I'm that close to my father, but because he was my last chance to stay here in New Hope. To stay with William.

"Have you packed yet?" Drew asks me. "Are you excited? Do you think we'll get to see the lights in Vegas? How long will the drive take? Can I take my Barbies?"

Her questions nearly shatter me. Even if I could talk my mother into letting me stay here without her, I know I can't do it. Mom's just a couple of orange pill bottles away from being an unfit mother. My sisters need me.

I can't put it off anymore. I need to tell Will.

The birds sing the whole walk to his house. Their happy tune contrasts so painfully with the dull knife sawing through my heart that I just want to close my eyes and listen until their hopeful song fills my ears and my head.

Will's car is in the driveway, and I don't ring the bell. I go to the back of the house and through the mudroom door he keeps unlocked when he's home. His grandmother is in Indianapolis visiting her cousin this week, and he made it clear I could come over any time I wanted. Made it clear that he'd like me to stay over. Why haven't I? What am I waiting for?

The mudroom leads to the kitchen, and I find a banana peel and an empty cereal bowl, milk lining the bottom, on the counter. He must have made a snack after getting home from track conditioning.

I head to the front of the house and find him on the couch, hair wet, bare from the waist up, and sleeping. One hand is behind his head. The other rests on his abdomen, right over that faint trail of hair that marks a path from his chest into his sweatpants.

Between football and track and general self-discipline, Will pushes his body hard, and he exhausts himself in the weight room.

I approach the couch quietly and lower myself to my knees on the floor beside him. He'd want me to wake him up, but I want to look at him first, memorize the shape of his chest and the flat of his stomach, the way his thick blond lashes curl against his cheek, and the untamed curl of his hair.

Before I realize what I'm doing, my hands are on him, tracing down his body, following that path of hair to the waistband of his sleep pants. I've touched Will before. I've given him massages, put my lips to the bare skin of his back, kissed my way down his spine while my hands rubbed at his sore muscles. I like massage. Despite the ugly things Mom has done to her massage business, I admire the art of human touch. With William, massage feels like this gift I can give him.

He shifts, and I lift his hand from his belly and start to work my thumbs into his palm. I work my way up to his forearm, and he moans appreciatively in his sleep. I stroke his arm, kneading the shoulder and the bicep, keeping my touch light and easy. When I finish his arm and he's still sleeping, I straddle him and start on his chest. His pecs are always so tight, and he shifts under me when my fingers press into those muscles.

I shift to catch my balance, and when I settle back down, the hard length of his erection is settled right between my legs. I draw in a breath at how good it feels and flick my eyes back to his sleeping face.

I've wanted to touch him for so long now, and I've been too self-conscious. This could be my last chance. I could be leaving at the end of the month. Will wanted us to keep seeing each other while he went away to college, but the nearly two thousand miles between New Hope and Las Vegas is a far cry from the few hours between here and Notre Dame. We'll be lucky if we see each other a couple of times a year.

The thought tears through me savagely, and I swallow a sob. I'll anesthetize the pain of the future with the beauty of the moment.

I shift back and lower my head to his chest, following the same path my fingers just took with my mouth and kissing my way down that downy-soft hair on his belly. When I reach his waistband, I lift my head to see him staring at me. His chest rises and falls in a rhythm faster than his sleeping breath and his blue eyes have gone smoky. I don't say anything, just lower his pants down his hips with a light tug.

He isn't wearing underwear beneath his sleep pants, and my breath catches at the sight of him. I've felt him before—between my legs and through our clothes—but I'm still surprised at his size. But it turns me on too. Seeing how aroused he is. Knowing he's watching me. That he wants this.

I put my hand around him, a little unsure and awkward at first, but then he groans—long and low—and I'm emboldened and tighten my hold. I lift my eyes to his face again as I stroke him and he's still watching me with heavy lids and parted lips. The pleasure on his face is the most beautiful thing I've ever seen.

I've been afraid of becoming my mother. Afraid that sex with William would destroy everything. I underestimated us.

"Jesus," he hisses at the first touch of my tongue. "Cally."

I might not have done this before, but I've read enough issues of *Cosmopolitan* to have an idea how it's supposed to go.

Before long, his hands are tangled in my hair and his moans of pleasure fill my ears, and I'm saying a silent prayer of thanks to all those *Cosmo* articles.

William

SHE'S CRYING. I'm not sure what I did wrong, but it must have been terrible because one second she was snuggling with me on the couch after giving me the most precious gift in the world, and the next her body was shaking and her tears were wetting my bare chest.

"Sweetie." I tuck her hair behind her ear and dry her wet cheeks with my thumb. "What's wrong?" Jesus. Is this about what she just did? Does she think that makes her like her mom? Should I have stopped her? "Talk to me."

She draws in a shaky breath, rolls off me, and walks across the room to look out the window. I follow her, my stomach churning and sour. I've never seen her this upset.

"I knew this couldn't last, but everything was going so well. Now she's ruining it all."

Her words terrify me. *I knew this couldn't last.* "You're not making sense. What couldn't last?" I already know she's talking about us, but I don't want to admit it to myself. I can't let myself belief she's ending this. Not now.

She presses her palm against the glass. "We're moving."

Those were the last words I expected to hear, and at first they don't even make sense to me. "What?"

"To Las Vegas. We're moving to Las Vegas."

I feel like the earth has just been yanked out from under my feet, but I make myself take a deep breath. Turning her around, I look into her eyes. "Start from the beginning."

"Mom and Dad are getting a divorce, and Mom's taking us to Vegas to live with this guy she met online." Her voice shakes and her eyes brim with tears.

I slide her hand into mine, interlocking our fingers and squeezing. "Can you stay with your dad?"

She shakes her head, and a tear spills onto her cheek. "He's going on some spiritual journey in Asia. He's already left."

"You can stay with me," I blurt. God, my grandmother would pitch a fit, but I ask for so little, and we could make it work. Somehow.

Cally shakes her head. Another tear escapes. "My sisters. You know my sisters need me. Mom's cleaning up, but what if that doesn't last? What if…" She squeezes her eyes shut and her chest shakes with her tears.

I gather her against my chest and smooth her hair. "Shh," I whisper. "Shh."

I guide her back to the couch, where I pull her into my lap and hold her.

I keep my thoughts to myself and let her cry. She needs this as much as I need to hold her, to feel her in my arms while I still can.

My brain is scrambling to come up with reassurances, plans for how we're going to make this work—because there's no alternative. We *are* going to make this work. Anything else would be like rejecting a piece of me. She's my heart, my breath.

We're connected. Tied together by something bigger than ourselves. Like the moon brings the tide back to the shore, the stars will always bring me back to Cally.

chapter nine

William

HER ROOM is empty. Her walls are bare, the posters and knick-knacks taken down and packed into the boxes now filling the moving truck parked in her driveway. Her dresser and bed are gone, and her chair and reading lamp with them.

All that remains is a makeshift sleeping spot on the floor, a small pile with tomorrow's clothes, and a tiny toiletry bag.

The sight tears me right in two, but I don't let on how much I'm hurting. I can't. I've done everything to make the most of our last weeks together, and tonight will be no different.

"You should get home," she says. "Get some sleep."

We've been sitting here most of the night, cuddled into the corner of her room listening to NIN on my iPod. I don't intend on going anywhere without her tonight, and I certainly don't intend on sleeping.

Her mom announced they'll be leaving at sunrise, and I won't miss a second with her.

I stand. "Come with me."

She takes my hand and follows me out the front door. I can't take another moment sitting in that house, watching her eyes scan the bare walls, the empty closet, the spot where the bed used to be. Besides, I have a surprise waiting for her.

Hand in hand, we walk to town and behind the old factory and onto the dock. I have everything set up for us here. We've made a habit of this since our anniversary. Blankets, candles, strawberry wine. From the moment she told me she was moving, I knew this is how I wanted us to spend our last night together.

She gasps when she sees it, her steps slowing. "You didn't have to do anything like this."

Thunder rolls overhead. The whole weekend has been gray and gloomy, only threatening rain. I say a silent prayer that the downpour that's sure to come will hold off until morning. I planned for stars. That's all I wanted for her. For us.

I light the candles and open the wine. The crystal goblets I snagged from my grandmother's hutch glint in the candlelight.

Cally shivers and lowers herself onto the blanket across from me. She avoids my gaze as she sips the wine, and I know she's trying not to cry.

"I have something for you," I say softly. I grab my backpack from where I'd stowed it by the edge of the building and pull out a small red box wrapped in white ribbons.

She takes it carefully. "You shouldn't have."

"Just open it."

She pulls at the ribbons with shaking hands and takes off the lid. I hear the catch in her breath when she sees what's inside. "But I won't be here," she whispers.

"Yes, you will," I promise. "One way or another, I'm going to get you here. I don't want to go to prom with anyone else, Cally. I want to go with you. Tell me you're on board with that. Tell me I can look forward to dancing with you in my arms."

Her face softens and her shoulders sag as she drops her gaze back to the prom tickets in the box. "Of course. We'll make it work," she whispers. And relief rushes through me like fresh air because I know she's talking about more than prom.

Cally

THE NIGHT sky is dark with thick rain clouds, blocking the clouds and clogging up my throat as I try to prepare myself to say goodbye. "I can't see the stars."

He turns my face to his. The candlelight flickers in the wind and casts shadows across his gorgeous face. I've been living a dream with William. Over a year of a life I never thought I'd get to live, receiving love I didn't realize existed.

He presses his lips just below my ear and trails kisses down my face. I melt a little, my defenses falling when I need them most. "We don't need them tonight."

I wish he were right, but I feel like a wish and a dream is all we have. How many high school sweethearts stay together? A few, maybe. But how many high school sweethearts weather the storm of a long-distance relationship and stay together? Maybe in movies. But this is real, and William deserves more than some long-distance girlfriend.

"She's being so selfish, taking us away from our life here. Taking me away from you." I sound petulant even to my own ears, but it's as if I believe giving voice to my frustrations will fix them. Not true.

William's eyes narrow. "Don't give up on us." He smoothes my cheek with his thumb. "She can make you move, but she can't take you away from me. You're mine. In New Hope, in Nevada, in Timbuktu, you'll always be mine."

He rolls over so he's hovering over me, his body on mine, his hips pressed to my hips, and he traces the lines of my face with his fingertips. My jaw, my cheeks, my lips. Despite all his bravado, he knows this is goodbye.

I pull him down to me, press my lips to the side of his neck, his jaw. "Can we really survive a long-distance relationship?" I hate how much I need his reassurances, but I want to hear them. Because even if he's wrong, his belief in us is the only thing that's getting me though this.

"It'll only be long-distance when we're apart. You'll be back for prom. We'll see each other this summer."

"Prom." The prom his grandmother wanted him to attend with some rich friend's daughter. Instead, he's holding out for me. How selfish have I been? He should be with someone better, someone *here*.

He slides his hand into my shirt and brushes my breast with his thumb. The single touch sends shivers of pleasure through me that gather in a needy knot of impatience between my legs.

"Prom," he repeats. "Just like we planned. Then when school starts, you can visit me at the dorms."

And always be scraping for money to buy my next plane ticket or, worse, letting him pay my way time after time. "You deserve better." But as I say it, I part my legs, wanting to feel him there where I ache. He brings up his knee until his thigh is firmly pressed between mine, and I moan against that delicious pressure.

"There's nothing better than you."

I blink back tears. "I don't want to wait for prom night," I murmur. Because I know now what I need to do. What I need to give him. "I'm ready now."

His nostrils flare and his eyes darken. "Are you sure?"

I wiggle under him and wrap my legs around his waist. I feel him pressing into me. I have to do this. I should have done it a long time ago.

A tear slips from my eye and rolls down my cheek, and he freezes. "Not tonight. Not while you're so sad."

I feel like I've already lost him. "So this is what goodbye feels like."

"No," he growls, and his fingers tighten their hold at my sides.

"We have to say goodbye. I leave in a few hours."

With his thumb against my cheek, he wipes away my tears. "We aren't going to say goodbye because this isn't the end of us. It's only the beginning."

Squeezing my eyes shut, I just lie there while he kisses away my tears. "If we don't say goodbye," I whisper, "then what do we say?"

"Look at me." His voice is firm and strong, but his eyes are soft when I look into them. "This isn't goodbye."

"We can't pretend that everything is going to be the same."

"Hello, Cally."

"William—" The intensity of his love breaks my heart. Because even if he can't see it, I know what's coming. I'll be in Las Vegas and he'll be here. It will be fine at first, but then his grandmother and his friends will pressure him to spend more time out. Eventually he'll meet someone, because that's what happens to amazing people. They fall in love with other amazing people.

"It doesn't need to be the same," he says. "I love you, and I'm telling you hello. Hello, Cally."

The candlelight catches on a tear on his cheek, making it glisten for a fraction of a second before it falls away. Maybe I'm not the only one who understands what we're up against.

Wrapping my arms around him, I pull him to me and he buries his face in my neck, his breath hot and a little shaky. And because I can't bear his sadness, I whisper, "Hello."

THE END

This is the end of Cally and William's prequel, but it's not the end of them. Follow them when they're reunited seven years later in Wish I May. *You'll find the opening chapter on the following pages.*

chapter one

Cally

"IN ONE hundred feet, turn left onto Dreyer Avenue," my GPS instructs.

I inch forward, peering out my windshield and scanning the manicured lawn to the left for any sign of a road where there is nothing but grass.

"Recalculating," the computerized voice tells me. Her tone suggests frustration with my inability to follow simple instructions. "In one hundred feet, take a U-turn, then turn right on Dreyer Avenue."

"There is no Dreyer effing Avenue." I pound on my steering wheel. This is the fifth time since I returned to Middle-of-Lots-of-Cornfields Indiana that the fucker has tried to turn me into someone's yard. Thirty minutes ago, she repeatedly directed me to drive right into the damn river. Good thing I decided to drop the girls off at the hotel when we got to town, lest they see their big sister go homicidal on an electronic gadget.

Yanking at the wheel with unnecessary force, I pull the car over and throw it into park. My chest is tight and my eyes burn with tears I swore I wouldn't shed today. I made it through the last month without crying. I won't cry now.

It's bad enough that I've been reduced to this. Bad enough that I have to rely on my estranged father at all. Bad enough that I have to track his hippie ass down since he's too goddamned paranoid to carry a cell phone. But here I am.

"*You shouldn't hate him so much,*" my mom told me six months ago. "*He hasn't had an easy life.*"

"*I don't hate him. I'm ambivalent.*"

But that was before Mom's "heart attack" (code for *drug overdose* that may or may not fool my sisters). That was before the funeral and the grief and the bills. That was before my life disintegrated around me, as if it were built of nothing but dust.

I'm exhausted, one sister hates me and the other isn't speaking, and my ass is sore from being stuck in this car.

Fresh air. That's all I need. Then I'll follow the road back toward the highway and ask a gas station attendant for help.

I unbuckle and step out onto the paved street. God, it feels good to stretch.

I can't get over how *green* everything is. It's as if I've forgotten the color can exist in nature. The scent of cut grass is almost as rejuvenating as a solid night's sleep for my state of mind. The air is warm and sticky, and children are playing in the sprinkler on a front lawn down the street.

I remember doing that as a kid. Before the move. Before the end of our world as we knew it. Is it too late to give my sisters a chance at that childhood?

Doubt lodges like a soggy lump in my throat.

"Can I help you?"

I snap my head up, startled. "No, I'm good. I—" My eyes connect with the owner of the voice, and I lose my capacity for speech.

"Holy shit." The Adonis from my past narrows his eyes. "Cally?"

The sound of my name on his tongue catapults me back in time and suddenly I'm sixteen again, his cool cotton sheets sliding against my skin as his fingertips trace the line of my jaw, the hollow of my neck, the curve of my hip. I'm sixteen again and licking sweet strawberry wine from his lips.

Time has been kind to William Bailey. Bare-chested and glistening with sweat, he has an iPod strapped around his thick biceps and a T-shirt tucked into the side of his running shorts. He's bigger than he was at eighteen, more built, which is saying something since he was New Hope High School's star football player back then. My gaze drifts south but gets snagged at the ripple of his abs and the trail of blond hair disappearing into the band of his shorts.

Sweet Jesus.

The sound of him clearing his throat has me yanking my eyes back up to meet his.

"Look at you. You're all grown up." He grins, and my knees go a little weak. How could I have forgotten the effect this man's smile has on my knees?

"I could say the same for you." I bite my lip. Hopefully no drool has escaped.

That knee-killing grin grows wider. I'm toast.

This isn't what I expected. Not that I expected anything from William. I *hoped* to make it through my few days in town without seeing him, but of course not. Here he is. Looking for all the world like he's actually glad to see me when he should hate me.

"You live here? I mean around—" *Shit.* How am I supposed to construct a coherent sentence while looking at his bare chest? And that's not even taking into account the memories flooding my mind at the sight of him. I may have never had sex with him, but I have enough memories of doing *everything else* to rival even the most creative fantasies.

Shifting my gaze to those deep blue eyes is no better. A girl doesn't forget those eyes watching her as their owner slides his hand between her legs for the first time.

I study the ground and wave a hand to indicate the spot where Dreyer Avenue definitely is *not.* "I'm looking for my dad."

"You're in the wrong neighborhood." His voice has that low, delicious treble that makes my insides shimmy.

When I sneak a peek up at him through my lashes, I catch him studying me with his own assessing gaze.

I can imagine what he sees. We've been on the road for two days, pulling off only for gas and restroom breaks. We stopped in Kansas last night so I could get a few hours of sleep, and then it was back in the car at four a.m. for another full day today.

I would categorize my ensemble as "road trip chic." My snug-fitting black yoga pants end just below my knees, and I'm wearing a T-shirt that says *Peanut butter jelly time!* The outfit is topped off with bright orange flip-flops and the ponytail I threw my hair into this morning.

So, you know, the exact outfit I *wouldn't* have chosen to be wearing for a reunion with my first love.

I lean into my car for the scrap of paper with Dad's address and shove it into William's hand. "Can you help me find this?"

He doesn't look at the paper but frowns at me. "Seriously? You're lost?" He pauses a beat. "In New Hope?" His tone suggests that I've gotten myself lost in a paper bag. And, okay, New Hope *is* pretty damn small, but I haven't lived here in seven years, and it's changed a lot. The good areas are all run down now, the factories are closed, and the vast expanses of open land by the river have been developed into fancy neighborhoods with yuppy McMansions so ostentatious I can practically smell their oversized mortgages.

"My GPS keeps trying to get me to drive into the river."

At least that wipes the scowl off his face. "Yeah, GPS systems haven't kept up with the developments around here real well." He rubs the back of his neck, and the movement sends the muscles in his arm and shoulder flexing. Between his sweaty muscles and my memories, I'm pretty sure my panties have all but disintegrated.

I clear my throat and resort to asphalt-gazing again. How hard is it to put on a shirt? "If you can point me in the right direction, I'll get out of your hair. I'm sure I'm the last person you wanted to see today."

His grunt has me looking up at him again. Those blue eyes, those crazy blond curls. That mouth. "Cally..."

I sink my teeth into my bottom lip as our gazes tangle. He takes a step toward me, and he's so close, I have to lift my chin to keep my eyes on his, have to curl my fingers into my fists to keep from touching him. He's sweaty and solid and so damn gorgeous.

I wait—for him to tell me how horrible I am for what I did to him, for him to ask me why I did what I did. I don't know what I'd say. It's hard to imagine that, once, leaving New Hope—leaving William—seemed like the worst thing that could happen to me. I was so wrong.

But he doesn't ask and he doesn't move away from me. His gaze dips to my lips for the briefest moment, and the way my body responds to his nearness, even all these years later, even after...everything...it only confirms what I suspected.

After seven years. After the lamest breakup in the history of breakups. After breaking his heart and dismissing my own, I'm still very much *his*.

William

CALLY.

I can hardly breathe. My brain doesn't have time for something as trivial as oxygen when it's so busy cataloguing her features, memorizing the exact shade of her mocha eyes, warring with the anger and regret that have sprung to life as if they never left me to begin with.

I never thought I'd see her again. I didn't think I wanted to.

The moment I step closer, I realize my mistake. Being near her is like a sip of water to desert-parched lips. It whips something through me—memories, lust, first love. *Heartbreak.* She tilts her lips up to mine, and I actually think for one goddamned ridiculous minute that I might kiss her, that I want to. That I would swallow all my pride and forgive her for just one taste.

I step back before I can give in to the impulse, and her cheeks blaze to life, her blush as cute as the rest of her. That's the word for her: cute. Sweet smile and peppy ponytail, she exudes cuteness.

Except her ass. Her ass doesn't even land in the same stratosphere as cute, and those tight little pants do nothing to hide its soft, round curves. And her breasts. There's definitely nothing *cute* about the way her T-shirt stretches across their fullness. Or her go-for-miles legs. Not to mention the narrow strip of skin exposed between the hem of her shirt and waistband of her pants. Just looking at the single inch of flesh below her navel, and I practically taste strawberry wine.

Moonlight. Her warm skin under my tongue. The sound of her moan as my mouth dips lower.

The memory grabs hold of my senses and won't let go.

Fuck. I can't even lie to myself. Nothing about her says *cute.* Everything about her says *sex.* And *mine.*

"Directions?" she asks. "To my father's house?"

"Do you want me to walk you there? It's close."

I immediately regret the impulsive suggestion. I should be giving her directions, putting her in the car, and sending her back out of my life. But I want to be close to her for a minute, to prove to myself that I'm bigger than a seven-year-old shit breakup.

Or I want to prove to myself she's more than just a dream.

She worries that plump bottom lip between her teeth because, obviously, she's trying to torture me. How can I want her so much when I thought I hated her?

"I don't bite, Cally."

She mutters something I can't quite make out. It kind of sounds like "Damn shame," but I can't be sure because she's grabbing her purse and avoiding my eyes.

"Are you staying long?" I ask as we start walking. My voice sounds too damn hopeful and I hate that, but what are the chances she'd show up here again, let alone find herself lost right in front of my house?

She's here to see her dad, I remind myself. That shouldn't come as a surprise, but as far as I know this is the only time she's been back since she moved away.

"No. Not too long. Maybe a couple of days. I…my mom died, and I need to get my sisters settled in with my dad."

I stop walking and turn to face her, all my bitterness and aggravation falling away.

She's looking at the ground, those worry lines making an appearance again. I grab her hand and squeeze. "I'm sorry." I don't ask what happened. Having lost both of my parents when I was a kid, I know how quickly that question gets old.

"Me too."

We both know there's not much else to say, so we walk instead. She follows me, and we cut through my yard to the paved path down by the river. I resist the urge to point out my house, to show her how well I've done for myself. It would be mostly a lie anyway.

"So you still live here in New Hope?" she asks softly.

"I came back after undergrad."

"Anybody else stick around?"

I narrow my eyes at her. Does she already know my screwed-up history with the Thompson family, or is the question sincere? "Some of the guys from the team—Max, Sam, Grant. And all the Thompson girls except Krystal. She just moved to Florida with her boyfriend last month."

The mention of her old friends brings a smile to her lips and lights up her face, making her look like her old self. "Lizzy and Hanna are in town?"

"You should see if you can hook up with them before you leave. They'd love to see you."

She doesn't reply, but there's something about the way her face changes that tells me she's not going to seek them out. I wish I didn't need so badly to understand why. Cally didn't want to leave when her mom moved her away. She didn't want to leave her friends or her family. Didn't want to leave the life she had here. She was determined to keep in touch with us all, even talked about coming back here for college. She hadn't been gone but a couple of months when all that changed, and suddenly she would have nothing to do with any of us. Even me.

Arlen Fisher's cabin is along the river just off New Dreyer Avenue. The original road was closed in favor of creating some common green space for the new construction. This, of course, was code for putting some distance between the old rough neighborhood and the ritzy new one.

When I point to Arlen's house from the trail, she frowns.

"It's really...small."

Her dad's a rough man. Simple to the extreme. His cabin sits in the trees just beyond the flood zone. It's small, no-frills, and falling apart.

"Are you nervous?"

She's slowed her steps, consciously or not. "I've only seen him a handful of times since we moved."

That surprises me. Someone would have told me if she'd been back, as there aren't exactly secrets in this town, but I would have expected that her dad took trips to Nevada to see all three of his girls. "Really?"

She shrugs. "It wasn't what we intended, but things just never worked out. You know my dad. He has other priorities."

I remember, vaguely. The man liked books and studying religious texts. He liked to spend his time meditating and his money visiting psychics and spiritual leaders. "That sucks."

"The road goes both ways," she says, and I don't know if she's reminding herself of her own responsibility to the relationship or his.

"How do your sisters feel about moving back here?"

She leans over and picks up a gnarled tree branch. It's as long as her legs, and its beautiful knots stand in contrast to the smooth skin of her hands. I already wish I had my camera.

"He sent me my ballet slippers," she says softly. "After he found out about Mom's death. I didn't even know he had them, and they showed up in this package—these tiny little slippers Mom and I had picked out together before my first lesson." Her lips curve in a smile. "I was only five, and I remember him telling me, 'If you want to be a ballerina, just believe you will be.' It was always that simple with him."

Once, it was that simple with Cally, too. I was drawn to her because that unfettered optimism radiated from her. After spending my formative years in my cynical grandmother's house, Cally was a breath of fresh air.

I look up at the house. The sun has dropped in the sky, and the little cabin looms darkly in the shade of the trees. "Are you ready?"

"I think so."

"Want me to wait here?" Again, I surprise myself. I should be itching to get away from her, from the reminder of what she did to me, but it all seems so long ago and unimportant under the pall of the crappy last couple of years. And next to the news of her mother's death, my old resentment seems downright trivial.

Her shoulders drop with her exhale. She's nervous. "Thanks."

She maneuvers through the trees and up the steep wooden stairs to the house. After knocking on the door twice, she turns the branch in her hands, waiting, fidgeting, while I wait in the trees. This whole thing should feel much more awkward than it does.

She knocks again, leaning forward this time to peek in the window.

Two minutes later, she gives up and heads down the stairs.

"Y'all looking for Fisher?" someone calls when Cally reaches me.

Cally perks up. "Yes. Do you know when he'll be home?"

I recognize Mrs. Svenderson from my grandmother's beauty parlor. She swats away gnats as she moves toward us. "Dunno when," she says. "He just left, so I 'magine it'll be a few days, least. Usually is."

I watch Cally as she digests this. Emotions flash across her face one by one—disappointment, sorrow, frustration, and finally anger, settling in around her jaw and eyes.

"Thanks. I appreciate you telling me."

"I thought you were too good to come visit your old dad," Mrs. Svenderson says. "What's brought you here now?"

Cally gives a polite smile but doesn't answer the question. The old women around here don't beat around the bush. They figure life's too short, I guess, and ask what they want to ask.

"It's nice to meet you," Cally says, as if the woman didn't just insult her. "Thank you for your help."

When she reaches my side, we turn together and make our way back along the river.

"Did he know you were coming?"

"He knew." Again, anger flashes in her eyes, and it looks comfortable there, as if this Cally is angry a lot. The girl I knew wasn't like that, but a lot can change in seven years.

"Do you have a place to stay? Where are your sisters?"

"I dropped them at the little motel back by the highway. I wanted to make sure Dad was ready for us. They've had enough surprises lately."

What motel by the highway? "Wait. The Cheap Sleep?"

She shrugs. "Sounds about right."

Cally and her sisters certainly aren't living large if that's where they're staying. "You know people don't actually sleep there, right?"

She chuckles. I like the sound of it. It's not the girly laugh she used to have, but neither is it an adult's carefully crafted facsimile of a laugh. It's soft. Sweet. Honest. "We'll be fine. It's just for a few nights. Until Dad returns home and I can get them settled with him."

We walk in silence for a few minutes, the only sounds the rush of the river and our shoes scuffing against the paved path.

"Do you live around here," she asks, "or are you in town with your grandmother?"

When we cut back through my yard to her car, I nod to my house. "That's mine."

It's odd, seeing it through her eyes. I'm proud of the home I built—a two-story, brick behemoth with a gorgeous flagstone patio in the back— but as I watch her take it in, I'm almost embarrassed at the excess. Cally and her family never had much. In fact, they rarely even had *enough*. And now they're staying at the Cheap Sleep, and her dad is living in that dilapidated old cabin. Not much has changed.

She forces a smile. "It's beautiful. I'm very happy for you."

She steps away, but I grab her hand fast.

"Cally."

She turns to me, those big brown eyes, those perfect pink lips.

There are a hundred reasons why I shouldn't want anything to do with her, but I have two, maybe three days before she disappears from my life again. Maybe for good this time. I can't handle the idea of this being the end, and I'll be damned if I'm letting her stay at that shitty motel. "Why don't you and your sisters stay with me?"

She snorts. "You surely don't have room for us *and* your wife and two-point-four children."

"No wife. No kids. Just me and way too damn much space."

She shakes her head. "That's sweet of you, but we'll be fine. You've already done more than most would have." She walks to her car, slides into her seat, and pulls away without another glance my way, leaving me alone with my memories of strawberry wine.

Wish I May is available now.

other titles by
Lexi Ryan

New Hope Series
Unbreak Me
Stolen Wishes: A Prequel Novella
Wish I May

Hot Contemporary Romance
Text Appeal
Accidental Sex Goddess

Stiletto Girls Novels
Stilettos, Inc.
Flirting with Fate

Decadence Creek Stories and Novellas
Just One Night
Just the Way You Are

about the author

A *New York Times* and *USA Today* bestselling romance author, Lexi Ryan considers herself the luckiest chick she knows. Her books have been described as intense, emotional, and wickedly sexy. Lexi herself has only been described using two of those adjectives (feel free to guess but she's not telling). When not writing, she enjoys watching football, perfecting her chocolate martini, and reading her way to the title of Biggest Romance Fangirl Evah. A former college professor, her biggest fears include faculty meetings and large stacks of ungraded freshman composition papers. She now writes full-time from her home in Indiana, where she lives with her husband and two children and their neurotic dog. You can visit Lexi at her website www.lexiryan.com or find her on Twitter @ writerlexiryan or Facebook at facebook.com/lexiryanauthor.

www.ingramcontent.com/pod-product-compliance
Lightning Source LLC
Chambersburg PA
CBHW020547130626
46552CB00007B/2782